COWBOY, TAKE ME AWAY

A Blazing Eagle Ranch 4

PEYTON BANKS

This book was previously featured in the boxset, A Country Temptation.

— PEYTON BANKS

BLURB

He's a broken cowboy in need of the love from a good woman...

Stan Larsen had trust issues. His ex-wife had done a number on him, so he threw himself into his work on the Blazing Eagle ranch. Hard back-breaking labor was just what he needed to erase the memories of her deception.

Maybe relationships weren't for him.

Until he met her.

Nasia Henry blew into his life like a deadly cattle stampede. Her smile and laughter brightened his days, making him feel something he once thought was lost. She filled his every thought and had him anticipating the future.

It all appeared too good to be true.

Then his past returned, reminding him of all the things he tried to forget.

But could he shake his past and trust again?

"Don't you love me anymore?" Stan asked. He ran a hand through his hair, feeling his heart shatter. He turned around and took a few steps away. A breath escaped him as he stared up at the sky with its multitude of colors. It was a beautiful sight and too bad he couldn't really appreciate it at the moment.

The sun would be rising soon, and he just didn't have it in him to go through this now. He spun around and narrowed his eyes on her.

How dare she.

Why now?

He had to get to work.

Not a sound came from her.

Stan stood with his hands on his hips and glared at her.

He stalked over to her and gave her a solid kick.

His truck of ten years was finally dying. They had an attachment. It was the first vehicle he had purchased. Laney, he had nicknamed her, was a used pickup truck he had bought right out of college. She had been with him through thick and thin.

Now was not the time for her to die.

He had been trying to hold on to her a little longer. He wasn't ready to buy a new one. Stan couldn't just go buy a truck. He had to find one that he connected with, could handle him and everything he threw at it.

The smoke drifted from under the hood, rising into the atmosphere.

No one was on the back country roads at this time of day. All of the sane people were still sleeping. Only ranchers and farmers were up at the crack of dawn.

Pulling his phone from his back pocket, he groaned. He didn't want to make this call right now, but he had no choice. He had to get to work.

Rashad, his coworker, lived not too far from him and could scoop him up. He considered Rashad a friend, but the guy had too much energy, and he'd just moved in with his fiancée, Yani. The guy was all smiles all day.

It drove Stan crazy.

He remembered that feeling of new love and being totally enraptured with a woman. Not too long ago, he had been just like Rashad. Newly married, prepared to spend the rest of his life with one woman.

Stan snorted.

Well, his bitch of an ex-wife made sure he didn't ever want to experience love again.

"Yo, Stan. What's up, buddy?" Rashad's voice came through the line.

"Mornin', Rashad. I need a ride," Stan admitted. He leaned against his truck and gazed off down the road.

"Laney finally gave up on you?" Rashad chuckled. The sounds of the radio were behind him. "Where are you?"

Stan told him where he was located. "When you turn the bend, just follow the smoke signal up in the sky."

"I'm not too far from you now."

"Appreciate it, man."

"Did you call a tow yet?" Rashad asked.

"Not yet. It's too early." Stan was familiar with the local towing company, Roadside Rangers. This was not his first rodeo when it came to his truck breaking down. He, Todd, and Kate Pritchard, the owners of the company, were on first-name basis. They probably even had Stan's number memorized by now. They didn't open until around eight. He'd call later and have them tow Laney to his house. "See you when you get here."

"Yup."

Stan slid his phone back in his pocket and opened the driver's door. He grabbed his duffle bag out the truck and sat it on the hood. He took the truck's key off of his keyring and left it in the cup holder. There wasn't a chance in hell that anyone would try to steal Laney.

Leaning against his ride again, he pulled his Stetson down farther on his head and prepared to wait.

The town of Shady Springs was small community that was safe and secured. People could leave their homes and cars unlocked with no worries anything would be taken. Crime was low, and it was a good community to raise a family.

Stan snorted.

When he and Victoria had got married, they had chosen the town of Shady Springs because she had grown up there. Stan was originally from Aurora and didn't have a problem moving down to Shady Springs. Victoria worked from home for an insurance brokerage firm, and he was hired on as a ranch hand for the Blazing Eagle Ranch.

Everything was perfect.

She was close to family and had a job she loved. He got the opportunity to work on one of the largest steads in the state. The Brooks family were wealthy and ran one of the most successful cattle ranches in the state of Colorado.

But then everything came crashing down around them.

And now his truck had died.

He just couldn't keep a woman.

An engine revving off in the distance brought Stan back to the present. Bright headlights were coming down the road toward him.

Rashad guided his truck over to the side of the road. The window rolled down, revealing Rashad grinning like an idiot.

"Need a lift?" he called out.

Stan shook his head and tried not to smile. His friend had entirely too much energy for it being this early. Stan tapped the hood of Laney before making his way over to Rashad's truck. It was a new model and was nice-looking.

Stan hated buying cars.

That's why he'd held on to Laney for so long.

"Morning." He crawled into the vehicle.

"You look like shit," Rashad remarked.

"Yeah, nice seeing you, too," Stan grumbled, slamming the door shut.

Rashad chuckled, guiding the truck back onto the road. The two of them were the lead hands on the Blazing Eagle Ranch. The Brooks brothers and their father, Jonah, had hired Stan and Rashad around the same time.

They had got along immediately, and Stan knew he could always count on Rashad to pull his weight around the ranch or even listen when Stan needed to get shit off his chest.

They rode in a comfortable silence, the radio playing good ol' country music.

"Parker is going be gone for about a week," Stan said. Parker, the eldest of the Brooks brothers, had recently married his fiancée, and they were taking a short honeymoon. With him gone, Stan and Rashad would have to step it up to help Wade and Carson.

"I know. This is why we're about to make a pit stop into town before heading out to the ranch," Rashad said. He turned down the road that led to town.

"For what?" Stan shifted in his seat. He wasn't in the mood for anything but hard, back-breaking labor that would leave him wanting to do nothing but shower, eat, and go to bed.

"You appear to be in a mood, so if I'm going to have to deal with your grumpy ass today, I will need a good strong cup of coffee." Rashad smirked.

"Whatever." Stan rolled his eyes. He could go for some coffee as well.

"Have you thought about dating again?" Rashad asked quietly.

"Nope."

"Look, maybe it would do you some good."

"I really don't want to talk about it."

"I thought I would make a suggestion. Every woman isn't like her."

Stan could feel his friend's eyes on him, but he refused to meet his gaze. Rashad knew about his failed marriage and had been supportive, but this was something his friend wasn't qualified in giving advice on. At the moment he was head over heels in love and figured everyone should be as happy as him and Yani.

There had been a time when Stan had believed in love, but thanks to Victoria, he no longer did.

He was going to have to stop thinking of her.

She'd apparently forgotten all about him before their marriage was even over.

Stan settled back and took in the scenery of downtown. Their little town had everything that was needed. Many people had settled in Shady Springs and opened businesses where mostly everything could be found.

Rashad parked the truck in a spot in front of the Shady Beans Café'. It had opened a few months ago, but Stan had yet to visit it. He usually got coffee at one of the other diners in town.

"Coffee any good here?" he asked, exiting the truck. He shut the door and met Rashad on the sidewalk. He wasn't really in the mood to try something new, but he wasn't going to be ungrateful to Rashad since he was giving him a ride.

"Best in town. Yani comes here. The owner is a friend of hers." Rashad led the way, opening the door to the café.

The heavy scent of freshly baked goods greeted

him. His stomach gave a little rumble. He hadn't had a chance to grab food, thinking he would have snagged something when he bought coffee.

The café was homey, with wooden tables placed around for patrons to sit and enjoy their food and drink. It reminded him of a log cabin. There was even a large fireplace on one of the main walls. It would be perfect in here in the wintertime if they lit a fire in it.

There were a few people ahead of them, giving Stan time to study the menu.

There were two baristas working behind the counter. Soft music played in the background, giving the place a light atmosphere.

Stan relaxed seeing a few things on the menu overhead. His stomach growled. Laughter filtered through the air. Stan's gaze landed on the woman whose infectious giggles captured his attention.

His heart skipped a beat.

She was drop-dead gorgeous. Her smooth brown skin was flawless, her dark hair in a ponytail cascading down the middle of her back. Her eyes were almond-shaped, and her lips were painted a bright red, making him want to taste them and see if they were as sweet as strawberries.

She had an apron on that was tied at the small of

her back and did nothing but highlight her hourglass frame. Her waist was tapered in, but her wide hips flared out. His hands itched to rest on them.

What the hell was wrong with him?

Shaking his head, he moved up in line.

"What food have you had from here?" Stan asked Rashad. He cleared his throat, feeling it constrict.

For a brief moment his gaze met that of the beauty. His breath caught in his chest, and it was as if he had forgotten to breathe. Her warm brown eyes held a mischievous twinkle in them.

"You can't go wrong with anything. The bacon, egg, and cheese croissant are good." Rashad pointed to a picture next to the menu.

Stan jerked his gaze away from the woman and turned his attention back to Rashad. He pushed his Stetson farther down on his head.

He was trying to not stare at her while she worked.

A few minutes later, they stepped up to the counter.

"Hey, Rashad." The beauty waved to him.

"Nasia, how are you?" Rashad jerked his head in a nod.

She walked over to them, switching spots with the young man who had been taking orders.

"I'll take their order, Tarek," she said. "Go make the other drinks for me, please."

"Sure thing, boss." The kid moved over and began working on the orders.

"I got the tab." Stan slapped Rashad on the back.

"You don't—"

"I do." Stan held a hand up, not going to take no for an answer. It was the least he could do for his friend.

Rashad ordered his coffee and a sandwich. Stan's heart was racing. He glanced back at the menu, finally deciding on what he would order.

"What can I get you, handsome?" Nasia's smile was wide and genuine.

"Nasia, do you know my buddy, Stan?" Rashad asked.

"No, I don't believe so," Nasia admitted. She tilted her head to the side as if to study him.

Stan had to fight to not fidget in place, her big brown eyes taking him in. Rashad made official introductions.

"How are you, ma'am?" Stan nodded to her.

"I bet you I can tell you what you are going to order." She grinned. She leaned against the counter and folded her arms in front of her.

"Really?" Stan's eyebrows rose high. This was going to be interesting.

"Yup, one look and I can tell what you will order." She tapped her finger on her chin and studied him. Her teeth nibbled on her lower hip, and she stood tall. She was a little thing, much shorter than his six-two frame.

"Have at it." He folded his arms in front of him, too, and met her stare.

"Grumpy. A cowboy. Jeans, no creases…I'd say large coffee, black." She slapped the counter, giggling.

Rashad barked a laugh.

Stan fought the grin threatening to burst out. It had been a while since he'd had a woman flirt with him, much less made him smile.

Divorce had left him bitter. He removed his hat and ran his fingers through his thick hair, then replaced it.

He was rusty when it came to flirting; hell, he was probably making a fool of himself.

But one look in her eyes and at her smile, Stan couldn't care less. She didn't have any rings on her fingers.

"Almost," he drawled. His lips lifted into a

lopsided smile. "I do like to put some cream in my coffee."

Nasia's eyes grew round, and her grin widened.

"Okay, cowboy." She chuckled. "Anything else?"

He added a sandwich to their order. He took out his wallet and pulled a credit card out to pay.

She took the card and completed the transaction.

"I'll be right back." She handed the card back to him, then tossed a wink his way and spun around to get their order.

"Smooth, man." Rashad nudged him with his elbow.

"What?" Stand asked, trying to appear innocent. He cleared his throat and put his card back.

"Nothing. It's good to see you smile," Rashad stated.

Stan shrugged and followed Rashad over to pick-up area. He peeked a glance back over to Nasia. She flew around getting their order prepared.

"She is single," Rashad said.

"Good for her." Stan tried to keep his face neutral. He didn't want to give away that the tiny bit of information Rashad had given him had his heart skipping a beat.

Maybe Rashad was right.

He couldn't let the divorce consume his life. Maybe it was time to take a chance and live a little.

"Here you fellas go," Nasia announced. She set their two coffees on the counter and reached for their sandwiches.

"Thanks." Stan handed Rashad his order. He turned back for his and found Nasia watching him. He picked up his items, and this time it was his turn to toss her a wink. "Have a nice day, beautiful."

❧   2   ❧

Nasia sat back in her chair and blew out a deep breath. She couldn't focus on the computer screen. She had a ton of work to do, and the only thing she could think about was Stan.

I do like to put some cream in my coffee.

His deep baritone voice still echoed in her head.

Hell, he could put his cream in her coffee any day.

She smirked.

His visit with Rashad had been the highlight of her day. His clear blue eyes had bored into hers. She bit back a sigh at the memory of him removing his hat and running his fingers through his thick hair.

Who told that man to be so damn sexy first thing in the morning?

He'd started out as a grouch, but she had won him over and was rewarded with his crooked grin. Her heart just about stopped at the sexy way his eyes had darkened when he'd leaned over onto the counter.

Nasia had to fan herself at the memory.

Yes, he had made her morning all the more brighter.

"Nasia Henry, get yourself together." She laughed.

She had an employee who had called off sick, so it left her and Tarik for a while until someone else could come in. Lucky enough, the morning rush came through until about eight. At the crack of dawn, she usually saw all of the ranchers and farmers stumble in looking for their pick-me-up.

Nasia could have hugged Sara when she arrived and jumped right into the craziness. Nancy was the midday person, and she blew in like a whirlwind. With the three of them running the counter, it allowed Nasia to go work on the business side of Shady Bean Café.

Nasia had poured her blood, sweat, and tears into her shop. It opened four months ago, and so far so good. The town had accepted the little café, and there was always a steady stream of customers coming in.

Nasia was born in Shady Springs and had moved away after graduating from high school. Her father had accepted a job in Denver, forcing them to relocate. Her and Yani had been neighbors before the move and had stayed in contact with each other.

When Yani had heard Nasia was wanting to open her coffee shop, she had recommended she come back to Shady Springs. According to Yani, the town was growing, and new businesses were helping it flourish. Nasia had been reluctant at first, but once she'd come back for a visit, it felt like home.

Nasia had packed up her Denver apartment after securing a place to stay in Shady Springs. She'd moved and hadn't looked back.

Within months, she had secured the space and began laying all of the groundwork to get her café opened.

She had a love for baking and coffee and she was so happy she was able to turn her passion into a successful business. Each day, her pastries and muffins sold out before noon came. She had compiled recipes that had been passed down to her from her grandmothers and even some she had found and tweaked.

She took pride in her homemade items on her menu.

Eyeing the computer monitor, she knew it was pointless to try to keep working. She glanced down at her watch and saw it was time for her to leave. Normally, she stayed until closing, but today she had a hair appointment.

Nasia closed the programs she had been working in.

"At least I got payroll done," she muttered. Tomorrow she could put in her orders for supplies the café would need. Shutting down her computer, she pushed back from her desk and stretched. She snagged her jacket from the hook on the back of her door and put it on. She hefted her purse up on her shoulder and looked around her office.

The life of a small business owner was filled with nothing but the establishment. There was always something to do, something to order or fix. Nasia also had fun with coming up with a baked goods 'item of the month.'

She had to think of what she was going to feature next month. This would call for her to pore through her endless recipes she had stored away to find the perfect item.

Later tonight, with a glass of wine, she'd figure it out.

Nasia left her office and walked through the café.

"Call me if you need anything," she said. "Tarik, you're in charge. I'm only down the street."

"We won't." Tarik grinned.

He was an amazing kid who had recently graduated from college. He had applied to work for her since he was unable to find a job in his field of study, criminal justice. Nasia had been surprised that he hadn't secured a decent position, but apparently most criminal justice majors ending up becoming police officers. He would be enrolling into the police academy soon.

"Just in case, I'm going—"

"Go. Get out of here." Sara pointed to the door.

Nasia giggled at her employees. She had the best crew. They were loyal and very good at what they did.

"Okay." Nasia held her hands up and headed toward the door. "I will see y'all tomorrow."

"And not a minute sooner," Tarik called out.

Nasia shook her head and exited the building. Her employees knew her too well. Briefly, she had thought of returning once Yani was done with her hair.

There was a slight nip in the air. Nasia was glad she had snagged her jacket. The shopping district her shop was located in was bustling with the afternoon traffic. The Pretty Parlor salon wasn't far, and Nasia opted to walk. She needed the steps. She had been in the shop since four-thirty this morning, and it was wonderful to breathe in the fresh air.

There were a few clouds in the sky, but the weatherman hadn't called for rain today, but there was no telling. This was Colorado, and the weather could be unpredictable. Most times weathermen said one thing, Mother Nature did the opposite.

She scanned the area, and her gaze landed on some of the storefronts. Lately, she had been working so much she hadn't had any time to shop. The only things she had been purchasing were supplies for the café.

Nasia promised herself she would take some time this week to explore some of the stores. A few of them had caught her eye.

Now, she had to focus on her hair. This was one luxury she allowed herself weekly. Yani had talked her into the sassy ponytail last week. It was time to take it out. She reached up and scratched her scalp.

Arriving at the salon, she entered with a wide smile on her lips.

"Hey, Nasia," Tiny called out from behind her chair. "Yani said to just have a seat in her chair. She'll be here in a second."

"Okay, thanks." Nasia waved to her and gave nods and smiles to the other stylists in the shop. The Pretty Parlor was the only salon in the town of Shady Springs focused on ethnic hair. Nasia loved coming here. It was where she learned all of the gossip of the town.

Not that she was nosey or anything, but listening to the stylists and clients talk was the highlight of her visit.

Nasia hung her jacket up in the coat closet. She took one of the salon's black robes, slid it on, and settled down in Yani's seat. She took out her phone and sent off a text to let her friend know she had arrived.

"Would you like something to drink while you wait for Yani?" Tiny asked.

"No, thank you." Nasia shook her head.

"I hear Nina Hunt will be performing in Denver," Jessie announced. She was very close friends with Yani. She was in the middle of dying a woman's hair.

Excitement at the mention of the mega R&B star

went around the salon. Nasia was a big fan of Nina and was immediately calculating if she could afford to try to snag tickets. Nina's tickets were never cheap, but the woman sure knew how to perform and make it completely worth it.

"I heard that, too," Erin said. She sat her flat irons down on her counter and pulled out a comb and teased her client's hair. "She's going on tour here in the States before heading all over the world."

"We have to go," Tiny said.

Nasia agreed. She was going to have to call her sister and see if she would want to go. Aleka, her identical twin, always had the better luck when it came to getting tickets for events. Nasia was the elder sister by five minutes and was extremely close with her twin.

Her sister lived in Aurora, but they would both make the drive to go see Nina.

She was worth a girls' trip.

"When do the tickets go on sale?" Nasia asked.

"I believe next month," Jessie replied.

"Perfect." Nasia brought up the internet on her phone and researched for ticket sales. The pricing wasn't too surprising. She made a mental note to herself to call Aleka and tell her.

"I'm back," Yani called out. She was all smiles and blew into the salon. "I'll be right with you, Nasia."

"Take your time." Nasia smiled at her friend.

Yani rushed past, taking her coat off and disappearing in the back. A few minutes later, she reappeared and stopped by the chair. "How did the ponytail hold up?"

"Pretty good," Nasia replied. She spun around in the chair and faced Yani. Her friend had a certain glow to her that Nasia couldn't put her finger on.

"Awesome. I'm glad I talked you into it." Yani grinned. She put her apron on and tied it behind her. "You are one stubborn customer."

"Well, you know I'm simple when it comes to my hair."

"It's time we spice up your life." Yani spun the chair back around and began undoing Nasia's hair.

"How's everything going with your boo?" Nasia asked.

"Amazing." Yani sighed. "I don't know why Rashad and I waited so long."

Nasia grinned. Anyone who saw the two of them together in a room would have recognized the sparks. Even when Nasia had visited a few times and he was around, she'd sensed the electricity between them.

Nasia bit her lip.

Should she ask Yani about Stan? Rashad had said they were friends, so there was a big chance Yani knew of him.

"Question for you," Nasia began. She was nervous asking around about a man, but she was a slightly captivated with Stan.

The memory of his smile still had her heart racing.

"Sure. What's up?" Yani removed the fake hair that had made up Nasia's ponytail. Her natural hair had been braided and hidden.

"This morning, Rashad stopped by the café and he had a friend with him." Nasia's gaze met Yani's in the mirror. "His name was Stan. Are you familiar with him?"

Yani paused combing out Nasia's hair and chuckled. "Yeah, we've met a few times. He's a little quiet. According to Rashad, he just went through a rough divorce."

"Who we talking about?" Jessie asked. She made no qualms she was listening to their conversation. "Stan Larsen?

Nasia should have known. Nothing in a salon was secret. Everyone had ears like a fox. Nasia might as well have been yelling her question.

"Yeah." Nasia laughed.

"He's a cutie. Wife is crazy, batshit crazy," Jessie said.

"Oh, you know them?" Yani paused what she was doing.

Jessie shrugged. "Unfortunately, in this town, we all know someone or at least their neighbor, and I know Victoria Larsen," she admitted. "She's friends with my sister, Lynn. From what I heard, Victoria got caught in the bed with Stan's best friend, Connor."

"About a year ago, right?" Tiny asked. "I remember it being the talk of the town. That bitch didn't appreciate her hard-working husband."

"I need a man like him. Working his ass off to provide for me. Stan was so in love with her," Erin, one of the other stylists, chimed in. She was in the middle of braiding her client's hair.

"Ain't that the truth," Tiny murmured.

Nasia filed what she was learning in the back of her mind. No wonder he was Mr. Grumpy Pants this morning. He was going through some shit.

But I made him smile.

"You interested in him? I hear he's still single," Jessie said.

"Oh, I don't know. I had never seen him around and was just curious," Nasia lied. She didn't want her business in the streets.

These women knew they really could gossip, and she didn't want to chance her interest being the talk of the salon when she left.

"Come on so we can wash your hair." Yani tapped her on the shoulder.

Nasia stood and followed her over to the sink and sat down.

Yani helped her settle back in the chair where her neck rested on the curve of the sink. "Comfy?"

"Yeah, thanks."

"If you want, why don't I invite Stan over to dinner and you come over, too?" Yani asked softly.

Nasia grinned.

Yani knew how her coworkers were and had apparently waited until they were out of earshot.

"Sounds fun."

"It would be like a double date. We could do game night."

"That sounds perfect."

Yani turned the water on and let it run until it was warm enough. Nasia settled back and relaxed, processing what she had heard about Stan and his ex-wife.

Maybe all he needed was a little joy in his life to help him get over his past.

Nasia was ready to volunteer as tribute.

❧ 3 ❧

Stan adjusted his hands on the steering wheel of his rental. It had been two days since he'd had to bum a ride from Rashad. His friend hadn't minded and had even dropped him off at the only rental agency in town after work. Lucky enough they had one truck.

It was nice.

Brand-new.

But not for him.

He would tolerate the vehicle until he could narrow down which one he wanted to purchase. This time he would go for a brand-new one with all of the bells and whistles. He had worked hard and deserved to have one good thing in his life that wasn't going to bail on him.

Today was going to be long day. With Parker out, the hands all had to pitch in. He and Rashad would be helping again to cover.

"I need some coffee," he groaned. Yesterday he had been at the ranch from sunup to sundown. His body was a tad bit sore, and today, it would be the same.

He headed into town and instead of going to his normal diner to snag his cup of joe, he found himself headed toward the Shady Bean Café.

He told himself the coffee and sandwich were delicious and he just wanted to go back.

Support the new business.

Yes, that was why he was pulling in the parking spot directly in front of the little café.

He must be crazy. Nasia probably flirted with all of the ranchers and farmers when they came into her shop in the morning. It would be good for business.

Stan was sure she was a nice woman who wanted to make sure her customers kept coming back.

He wasn't anyone special. He'd been out of the dating scene for years and didn't have the first clue how to even approach a woman. He and Victoria had met at college at a party.

The other day had just been pure coincidence. Other than that, he had no game.

Hell, it was why Victoria had left him.

"You're always at the damn ranch," Victoria had screamed. *"You don't own it. You're there so much, you forgot about your wife."*

Nothing had changed aside from coming home to an empty house. In the divorce, he had got the house but couldn't stay there.

The memory of finding Victoria in the bed with Conner was etched into his brain. So he put the house up for sale and was currently renting another one. Didn't make sense to buy a home with it just being only him.

But something had him killing the engine and stepping out of the truck.

Butterflies fluttered in his stomach, but he pushed down his nervousness. He readjusted his Stetson and made his way to the building.

He opened the door to the café and again, the delicious smells of baked goods attacked his senses. His footsteps carried him over to the register. Only one person was ahead of him. A young woman worked the counter with the same young man who had been there the other day.

Stan stared at the menu, wanting to try something else for breakfast. He couldn't guarantee he'd get a lunch today so he figured he might as well eat now.

Settling on what he would order, he stepped up to the counter when it was his turn. The older man before him moved over to the pick-up line.

"Hi, can I help you?" the young woman asked. She had a warm smile, and her name tag shared her name: Sara.

"Morning." Stan cleared his throat, trying not to share his disappointment that Nasia wasn't taking his order. "I'd like a large coffee. Black with cream, and a large oatmeal."

"Sure thing," Sara said.

He slid her his credit card once she tallied the order.

She handed it back to him with the receipt. "Are you dining in or taking it to go?"

Stan glanced around and saw a few patrons sitting down enjoying their meals.

"Here." This was definitely different from his normal routine. No eating alone in his home. At least he was in public and around other people who had to get up at the ass crack of dawn to go to work.

He walked over to the pick-up area to allow Sara to take the order of the cowboy behind him. Stan recognized him as a hand from one of the other ranches. Their gazes met, and Stan returned his nod.

"Here you are, sir," the young man announced. He brought Stan his order on a small tray. "Need any sugar or butter?"

"A few butter and sugar will be fine." Stan offered him a tight smile. He didn't want to appear 'grumpy' as Nasia had called him.

"Here you go." The kid came back over and dropped everything on the tray.

"Much obliged." Stan nodded and picked up the tray and eyed the restaurant. He made his way over to a corner table and sat. He doctored his oatmeal and took a taste.

It may be oatmeal, but he wasn't sure what they had done to it. It was the best tasting bowl of oats he'd had in a while. He reached for his coffee, and again, best damn coffee he'd had.

He officially had a new place to obtain his caffeine.

He continued his meal and brought his phone out of his pocket. He hit the news app and turned his attention to it.

The atmosphere of the café was quiet, calming, and he was actually enjoying himself. The two baristas behind the counter were funny and playful, joking around with the customers.

Nasia's smile and laughter brightened his day and made him feel something he thought he had lost.

Disappointment filled him that he didn't get to see Nasia again. He pushed it down and listened to the weatherman discuss his predictions. Today, they were moving cattle, and it would help to stay up on the weather.

"Well, well, well. Look what the cat dragged in," a familiar breathless voice said.

Stan's heart skipped a beat. He glanced up into a pair of pretty brown eyes.

Nasia.

"Morning, Mr. Grumpy." Her killer-watt smile stretched across her face. She was dressed in a dark short-sleeved V-neck t-shirt and a pair of skintight jeans. Today her hair was different. Instead of the long ponytail resting on her mid back, her hair was dark, straight, and flowed around her shoulders.

His mouth watered at the sight of her.

She stood by his table holding a small plate. She set it down next to his oatmeal and took the seat across from him.

"Morning." He sat back in his seat and looked at

the new item she had put in front of him. He jerked his head toward it. "What is this?"

"Well, here at the Shady Bean Café, I like to feature a monthly baked goods and I've been in the kitchen trying to perfect something for next month."

Stan watched her excitement spread through her. Her face brightened, and her hands moved around as she spoke. She had a passion for what she did, and it was refreshing.

"This right here is a strawberry shortcake muffin, and it's on the house." She leaned back and motioned for him to try it.

"Free?" His eyebrows rose. "What did I do to deserve a freebie?"

He reached for the oversized muffin. He tore it in half and saw the fresh strawberries baked into it. It was still warm with steam rising from it.

"Well, seeing how this is your second time here this week, I figured I would try to seal the deal of you becoming a regular here." She rested her chin in her hand, watching him take his first bite.

He closed his eyes and savored the sweetness of the muffin.

"You got something here," he murmured. He took another bite, reaching for his coffee and taking a long swig.

"You think so?" Nasia grew excited, dancing in her seat.

"I do. Woman, you have a gift," he said. He finished the muffin in two additional bites.

"So, do I have you as a faithful customer?" she asked. Her voice grew husky, and she entwined her fingers together.

He bit back a groan as he watched her teeth nibble on her bottom lip. It was plump, and he had the sudden desire to replace her teeth with his lips. He bet Nasia would be sweeter than the strawberries she used for her new muffins.

Stan blinked.

He set his coffee down and met her curious gaze.

"On one condition."

"Yeah?" She tilted her head and studied him. Her dark eyelashes fluttered against her cheeks. She reached up and tucked her dark hair behind her ear.

Yeah, she was flirting with him.

It didn't take a rocket scientist to recognize this. He cleared his throat, a little rusty at the flirting game. Nasia was a beautiful woman, blessing him with her attention and baked goods, so the least he could do was return the favor.

He titled his Stetson back and leaned forward,

resting his forearms on the small table. She moved forward toward him.

"I get to taste all of your experiments in the kitchen first."

"For you, anything, cowboy." She grinned and glanced over her shoulder at the baristas behind the counter then turned her attention back to him. "I have more in the back. I can pack them up so you could take them home to your wife and kids."

Her eyes grew wide, and he smirked.

"Divorced. No kids." Was this her way of trying to feel him out? Admitting his status was a bit easier than he would have thought. It had taken him a long time to come to the realization his marriage was over. He held up his hand. "No ring."

"Well, I've learned some people don't wear a ring and are married." She shrugged.

Her gaze dropped down to his hand. He held back covering it. Even with working long days on a ranch, he'd never taken his ring off. Now it had been off for a little over a year, and the faint hint of it was still on his finger.

"Not me." He shook his head. The sanctuary of marriage had been important to him.

But apparently it hadn't even mattered.

His still ended, and even though his wife was

fucking another man, she found a way to blame her indiscretions on him.

"What about yourself?" he asked. He busied himself by taking another sip of his coffee. He found himself near the end of it and didn't know how he had gone through the cup so fast.

"Never married. No kids." Her smile disappeared as they stared into each other's eyes.

Not married, no kids.

Good.

Now, was this the part where he asked her out?

Shit.

What the hell did he say next? He racked his brain, cursing that he was so out of touch with members of the opposite sex and the dating world. When he'd met Victoria, he had been much younger, in college, and dated around. Once they'd gone exclusive, he hadn't had to worry about picking up women.

Just providing for one who was ungrateful for all of his hard work.

Stan peered down at his phone and released a curse.

He had to go to work and had lost track of time. He hadn't meant to stay this long.

"Want a refill?" She motioned to his empty cup.

"Sure, but I have to take it to go." He pushed back from the table and stood, not missing the look of disappointment in her eyes before it disappeared.

Nasia stood and reached for his empty cup. "Black with a little cream, right?"

His lips tilted up into a grin.

She'd remembered.

"Please."

"Be right back." Nasia tossed him a wink and walked to the counter.

His gaze dropped to the swell of her ass, and he couldn't help but give it an appreciative glance. Her wide hips and supple ass in the tight jeans had his attention.

Stan tore gaze away from Nasia and cleared his table. He tossed his trash into the garbage and sat the tray on top of it. He turned and found Nasia walking toward him with a large cup.

"How much do I owe you?" he asked, taking it from her.

Their fingers brushed each other, and a small jolt of electricity traveled up his arm.

"Coffee refills for patrons who eat in are free." She backed away from him slightly with a little wave. "Have a great day at work, Mr. Grumpy."

"It's Stan," he said, not wanting her to forget his

name. He wasn't sure she'd remember it from the other day.

"Oh, I haven't forgotten." She smiled and turned, walking away.

Stan spun on his heel and marched out the café with a wide grin on his lips.

Today was going to be a good day after all.

❧   4   ❧

"**A**re you going to stand around on your phone making kissy faces at it or are you going to help me?" Stan snapped. He knelt on the ground near the fence, seeing a slight opening in it. He glanced around and didn't see any of the cows roaming on the outskirts of the Brooks property.

"Hold your horses." Rashad snickered. "I'm going to have to run up to the big house soon. Wade needs me to help transport a horse for him."

"Just help me real quick, and I should be good." Stan used his pliers to bend back the metal of the fence.

Rashad stepped over with a new wooden plank that would go into the hole they had widened to accept the wood. "Yani just texted me, and she was wanting to invite you over for dinner tomorrow. She wants to have a game night and suggested I should bring you," Rashad said. "A friend hers will be there, and we wanted to make it even."

Stan froze.

"Game night?" he asked, bringing the wire around the post. He saw right through the ruse. Rashad was trying to set him up on a blind date.

Stan had pride.

He didn't need someone to match him up with a woman.

He could do it on his own.

Eventually.

When he felt he would be ready.

"I don't know," Stan murmured. He grimaced, bending the wires to get them to hold. He quickly racked his brain to come up with any excuse he could to be able to get out of going. Rashad and Yani were good people, but all of the lovey-dovey display was more than he could stomach. "Look, Rashad. I appreciate your concern, but I'm fine. Victoria and I were together for a long time. I haven't been single since I was in college."

He sat back on his haunches and removed his

Stetson, tossing it on the ground. Rashad didn't say a word at first.

"I'm not saying you need to go out and marry someone. All I said is go out, mingle, get to know other women. You just got to get your feet wet. They all aren't like Victoria. She was a selfish bitch who didn't deserve you."

Stan eyed Rashad who was dead serious. It wasn't often Rashad didn't smile, and for him to be staring at Stan without a hint of a joke, it was little creepy.

But his friend was right.

Victoria had been selfish. Even in the divorce, she had tried to take him for everything he had, but lucky enough for him, his lawyer was top-notch and the magistrate saw through her lies and deception. She only walked away with half of their savings account, her car, and half of the items in their house. Stan hadn't cared about the material things, she could have had it all. He had just wanted to be done with her.

"Let me think about it," Stan started. He tunneled his fingers through his hair and glanced at the sky. Lucky enough, the clouds were holding. The weatherman had called for rain in the late afternoon. They had moved a herd of cattle from this sector to another to allow the land to recoup and for them to fix any of the fences the animals may have damaged.

"Nasia will be there."

Stan froze in place again.

"The girl from the coffee shop?" He cleared his throat and hoped Rashad didn't pick up on his excitement.

"Yeah, the woman you were flirting with the other day." Rashad nudged him with his elbow.

This could be the opening he needed to ask her out.

"Well, I mean, if you don't want her to be a third wheel, I can come." He didn't glance up at his friend, who he knew without looking was grinning from ear to ear.

"I'm texting Yani now to let her know you'll be there." Rashad chuckled.

Stan rolled his eyes and finished what he was doing. The post was stable and should hold for a while. He pushed up off the ground and snagged his hat, putting it back on.

"Should I bring anything?" he asked.

"Knowing Yani, the food will be taken care of. Why don't you bring something to drink?" Rashad shrugged.

Drinks, he could totally do that.

Cooking wasn't his thing. He could handle enough to keep him alive. He was a frequent at the local diners and restaurants, utilizing their carry-out options.

"Sure thing. What time?" Stan coasted a hand along his jawline and felt the bristles of hair he'd just let grow, uncaring about the beard.

"About seven." Rashad gave him a salute then jogged over to his horse, Brandy, who was grazing nearby. He quickly mounted her and trotted off.

Stan cleared the tools and walked them over to the ATV he had driven. Thoughts of Nasia hadn't been far from his mind. Now he would have a chance to see her again, this time away from the café.

"YOU SHOULD KNOW THIS!" NASIA screeched, tears running down her face. Her stomach hurt from laughing so hard. She motioned to the pictures on the white paper again with her marker.

Stan appeared bewildered.

"What is that?" He chuckled, a beer dangling between his fingers.

"Time!" Yani shouted.

Her and Rashad fell back onto the couch in a fit of giggles.

Nasia tucked her hair behind her ears and shook her head. The Stan she was seeing tonight versus the one she had first met were almost two different people. Gone was the dark shadow of a beard, his face was more relaxed, he even smiled often tonight.

The man looked damn good in jeans and a button-down shirt. His blue eyes twinkled with merriment.

"Seriously, you can't guess this?" She stomped her foot, resting her hands on her hips.

Stan pushed off the loveseat and walked over to her with his attention on her fabulous drawing. He stopped next to her, and the scent of his cologne reached her.

Her core clenched.

Why did he have to smell so tempting? She breathed him in and fought to keep her hands to herself.

He squinted at her picture.

"Is this a goat?" He motioned to the animal.

"No, a horse."

Yani and Rashad's cackling grew even more.

"A horse?" Stan chuckled. He raised the long-neck bottle to his lips and gestured to the other picture. "And this?"

"That's a man, and I'm pointing to his back."

Stan coughed, and she could easily see he was fighting to hold back his amusement. Nasia rolled her eyes and elbowed him out of the way.

"Horseback riding," Nasia moaned. She slapped her forehead in disbelief he didn't get something that should have been so easy for him.

Hell, the man was a cowboy, for Pete's sake.

He rode horses for a living.

Stan's gaze fell on her. His deep laughter softened her will to win. She was competitive by nature. Growing up with a twin meant there was always someone vying for more attention from their parents, someone wanting to be better at everything she did.

Nasia made the cheer squad in high school.

So did Aleka.

They both always got honor roll in high school.

College, pledged the same sorority.

They did everything together, and it was always a competition on who would do it better.

"What's wrong with my horse?"

"Next time, you may want to give it a longer tail, make it a little taller..."

"Most horses I've ridden and trained have manes." Rashad snorted.

Yani sat next to him with tears rolling down her face.

"It's okay, Nasia. You'll get it next time." Stan brought her flush against him, his arm wrapped around her waist.

She bit back a moan from the feeling of him.

"Why don't we go outside. Rashad can light the fire pit he just built for us," Yani mentioned. She wiped her cheeks and glanced around the room.

"We're not taking no for an answer. Yani's been dying to use it." Rashad stood and reached back to help Yani up.

They left the family room and disappeared into the kitchen. They had been the perfect hosts, good food, plenty of drinks, and the entertainment was hilarious. None of them were professional artists, so all of their pictures were childlike and hard to guess.

That's what made the game so enjoyable.

"Sure, sounds like fun," Nasia said. She looked up to Stan. He was much taller than her, and she had to tilt her head completely back to meet his gaze. "Is that cool with you?"

He hadn't removed his arm from around her waist, and she wasn't complaining. The entire night had been full of fun, jokes, and flirting. Every few moments, Nasia found her resting a hand on him, his arm around the back of the couch behind her. It was like they were a couple.

"Fine by me." Stan's voice rumbled deep in his chest.

Nasia's heart fluttered.

Everything just felt right.

Nasia turned into his embrace, brushing off an invisible piece of lint from his shirt. She took advantage of the move and rested her palm on the hard plain of his chest.

They stared into each other's eyes.

"This was nice," he murmured.

"It was."

"Almost better than the muffin you let me try out." His lips curved up into a sensual grin.

"Is that so?" She raised her eyebrows high.

His smile slowly dimmed, his hold on her tightening.

"Nasia…" He hesitated.

"Yes?" She leaned into him, waiting to see what he was going to say.

He studied her for a moment, and her body grew tense. Maybe he wasn't interested in her like she had thought he was.

Had she read him wrong?

"Look, I don't know what I'm doing. It's been so long since…hell, since I've felt this way about anybody," he admitted sheepishly. "But I like you. A lot. I was wondering if you wanted to grab a bite to eat sometime. Maybe this weekend?"

Nasia's heart swelled watching him stumble through asking her out. His gaze locked on her, and he waited for a response. His muscles were tense underneath her touch.

From what she'd heard about him, he was a true sweetheart and that ex-wife of his had taken advantage of him.

"I would love to." She smiled and casually stroked his chest. A gasp escaped her at the feeling of something hard pressing against her stomach.

Oh boy.

He was definitely big all over.

She didn't break his gaze but stepped closer to him, ensuring nothing could slide between them. Her core clenched imagining what it would be like with him. It had been a while since she'd been with a member of the opposite sex.

She was bold and definitely wanted him to know she was interested. Nasia wasn't going to hesitate in going after what she wanted, and right now, Stan Larsen was someone she wanted to get to know.

Intimately.

She would help him get over his shyness and second-guessing.

That ex-wife of his apparently did a number on him, and Nasia was volunteering to make everything in Stan Larsen's life better.

Her loss was Nasia's gain.

"Are y'all coming, or you going to stand in there making googly eyes at each other?" Rashad called out from the kitchen.

"We're coming," Stan shouted back. He chuckled, his grip tightening on her for a moment. "I swear he's the most impatient person I know."

"Let's not keep them waiting," she whispered. Her gaze dropped down to his lips, and the urge to lean up to kiss him was strong.

Would he be turned off by her boldness?

Stan took her hand in his and entwined their fingers together and towed her behind him.

She would have to wait for their first kiss.

There was going to be one.

Nasia was sure the sparks between them were only the tip of the iceberg.

Things with Stan would be explosive.

She could feel it in her bones.

Since he'd arrived, her body was going haywire. He nipples were continuous buds, his dark gazes left her panties soaked, and any time his hand landed on her, she just wanted to explode.

They exited the house through the kitchen doors that led to the stone patio. The fire was already burning, giving them some light. Yani had the patio specifically designed for entertainment. It was a curved area where stone seating surrounded the in-ground fire feature.

Them holding hands wasn't missed by Yani. A wide grin spread across her face. She winked at Nasia, leaning into Rashad. They took a seat across from Yani and Rashad.

Nasia was sure Yani was going to want details, but she wasn't talking until she had something good to share.

❀   5   ❀

"**T**his was fun." Nasia hugged Yani.

Stan stepped out of the house and turned to Rashad who was right behind him. The night had gone better than he had planned. There was definitely something between him and Nasia.

He'd have to be blind, deaf, and mute to not recognize it.

"Thanks for the invite," Stan said.

"No problem at all. Glad you could make it." Rashad's grin spoke volumes. He gave Stan a firm slap on his shoulder. "Now, I've led you to the water..."

Stan rolled his eyes at the idiom, but he got the

message loud and clear. He turned to find Nasia and Yani chatting. It was late, a little after midnight, and he wasn't ready for the night to end. They had sat out around the fire for some time, talking and laughing.

His attention had been captivated by Nasia, learning tidbits about her. She was goofy, smart, and headstrong. She had spoken about her decision to leave her district managerial job for a chain of coffee shops in the big city and move back to a small town to open up her own business. It took guts, and Stan had much respect for her.

It had been a long time since he had a regular night out with great food and friends. His gaze met Nasia's, and he nodded to her.

"See ya later." Stan gave Rashad a salute. "Yani, you have a good night."

"You, too, Stan. Thanks for coming." Yani waved, going back into the house with Rashad.

Stan followed Nasia down the stairs and over to her car. His truck was directly behind hers.

"It's late. Why don't I follow you home," Stan said, immediately pausing. He didn't know where this idea came from, but a protective nature came over him at the thought of her driving home so late. "Just to make sure you get there safely."

Nasia leaned back against the driver's door. Tilting her head to the side, she studied him.

"That would be nice. A woman can't be too careful in a small town." She pushed off the car and unlocked it.

"Just what I was thinking," he teased. He opened the door for her and helped her into her car.

A few minutes later, they were driving through town. Stan drummed his fingers along the steering wheel, guiding his vehicle behind Nasia's. The area they were in was not too far from Stan's home. It would take him about ten minutes to get to his house.

Soon, Nasia turned into a driveway, and he pulled his truck to the base of it. Nasia exited her car and walked over to his truck. He hit the button to lower the passenger window. She rested her forearms on the door and stared at him.

"Thank you for making sure I got home safely." Her voice was husky, his cock jerking at the sexy sound.

"Anything for you as long as the baked goods keep coming," he joked.

"Of course." She reached up and tucked her dark strands behind her ear. Her teeth snagged her bottom lip, and he could have groaned. Something so innocent was so damn sexy. "Would you like to come in?"

Stan froze.

She must have thought he was hesitating when in all reality he was just shocked at the request.

"I mean, I understand if you have to go to work tomorrow. I was just thinking, we were having so much fun at Yani and Rashad's that we could watch a movie or talk some more—"

"No, I'm off tomorrow," he interjected. This was his weekend off from the ranch for the month. He cleared his throat, running a hand through his hair. "I can come in. Let me pull into the driveway."

A wide grin spread across her face. She stepped back from the pickup and headed up the driveway to the front door. He parked next to her car and got out. By the time he arrived on the porch, she already had the door open and was standing on the inside waiting for him.

"Welcome to my home," she announced, waving him in.

"It's very nice." He closed the door behind him.

It was tastefully decorated and reminded him of a true home. His house had the bare essentials. When he'd moved in, decorating it was not at the top of his priorities. He had thrown himself into work and didn't care what the place looked like, and as long as it had a couch, a bed, a television, and a fridge, then he was good.

His gaze fell to her shoes by the entrance, so he toed off his boots, putting them next to hers.

"Can I get you something to drink? A Coke? Water?" She led the way to the living room. She set her purse down on the coffee table in the middle of the room. There were two plush couches with a huge television mounted on the wall above her fireplace.

"I'm good, thanks." He settled down on the couch nearest him.

Nasia smiled, sitting next to him.

"So what type of movies are you in to?" She reached for the remote. She flipped the television on, and a classic movie in black and white appeared.

Stan couldn't care less about the television, he had eyes only for Nasia.

She turned, finding him staring at her. "Or do you want to talk?"

"Um, talking is fine." He shrugged, unable to look away from her big brown eyes.

She tossed the remote on the table and fixed her attention back on him. She slid closer to him, pressing her body to his. His heart did a little flutter action, his cock stiff as a board pushing against his jeans.

Her hand slowly reached up and guided his face down to hers.

The second his lips brushed hers, he was a goner. Stan gathered her to him, his mouth plundering hers. Nasia wasn't shy at all, her tongue stroking his. A breathless moan escaped her, fueling the desire building inside him.

He dragged her on top of him to straddle him, her knees pressing onto the couch on each side of him. Her fingers slid through his hair, sending a shiver down his spine.

Stan rested his hands on her waist but then soon traveled up her torso, cupping her full breasts. He was a big man with large hands and her mounds filled his palms.

Nasia nipped his bottom lip with her teeth, eliciting a playful growl from him. She leaned back from him, her hooded gaze taking him in. She reached down and pulled his shirt from his jeans, then her fingers flew to his buttons.

Once she had his shirt open, a pleased sigh escaped her lips. She pressed hot openmouthed kisses to his jawline and trailed them down his neck and to his chest.

"Nasia," he gasped.

She paused and glanced up. His chest was rising and falling fast. He could barely breathe as he gazed down into her dark bedroom eyes.

"I haven't been with anyone since my wife." He cursed internally, a little embarrassed at the admission.

"It's okay." Her hand trailed along the ridges of his abdomen. "I haven't been with anyone in a while either."

"What I mean to say is my wife cheated on me. After finding out, I went and got tested. I came back clean."

Throughout their entire marriage, Victoria hadn't wanted to be on birth control. She had the excuse that she never felt right on it. So he had been the responsible one, wearing condoms with her until they decided they were ready to start a family.

The day never came.

Condoms.

Shit, he didn't have one. Hell, what was the point of buying them when he wasn't seeing anyone?

"It's okay, you don't have to explain." She slid down him and knelt on the floor in front of him.

He wasn't sure it was possible, but he got even harder. "I don't have any protection—"

"I'm on the pill." She smirked, reaching for his belt. Her hand paused, and she turned her big brown eyes to him. "Unless you don't trust that, then I understand."

He jerked his head. "I believe you."

She hadn't given him a reason to think she would be deceiving.

Nasia's sensual grin widened. Together, they wrestled him out of his jeans, sending them to the floor along with his boxer briefs. His cock sprang free, standing up at attention.

"Oh my."

Her hand grasped his shaft, and Stan instantly counted backwards from a hundred, thinking of all the football stats he could conjure. She took one long lick of him, and he had to fight to reach for her. He dug his hand into the cushion of the couch, and she took her first taste.

Her lips wrapped around the blunt tip, and he stiffened. His head dropped back, and she guided him fully into her mouth.

It was pure fucking heaven.

Her hand slid along the length of him in tandem with her mouth. Her tiny hand set a steady rhythm, leaving him panting. He needed to touch her.

He reached out and threaded his fingers into her

thick dark locks. Her throaty moan shot straight to his dick, and it was then he knew he wasn't going to last long.

Shit.

He tried to lift her gently, but she batted his hand away.

"Nasia..." He chuckled. He scrubbed a hand along his face, feeling the familiar sensation of his release. "If you keep that up, this is all going to be over before we even get started."

She flicked her gaze to his, and he bit back a groan at the sight of him in her mouth. She slowly released him. He leaned forward and snatched her up from the floor. He refused to allow their first time to be a one-minute fling.

Hell, no.

Not going to happen.

"Hey, I wasn't done." She laughed.

"You are for now," he muttered, making quick work of removing her clothes. She had entirely way too many on. The piles of clothing grew onto the floor.

Stan sat back and took in her full, high breasts, her dark areolas, her nipples beaded into tight buds, her waist tapered down to hips that flared out. Her body was like a Greek goddess, shapely, all womanly and currently his.

He was going to cherish every square inch of her.

He pulled her face to him and covered her mouth with his. It was a hard kiss, one where he wanted to consume all of her. She returned the kiss with a fire that left him wanting to bury himself so far inside her they wouldn't know where each other began.

They found their way to the floor. Stan braced himself over her, staring down into her eyes.

"You are so fucking beautiful," he murmured. He wanted to memorize every facet of her. He trailed a finger along her cheekbone, down to her lips, swollen from his kisses.

"As are you," she replied, a tiny smile on her lips.

He released a snort. He shook his head, then bent it down to press his lips to hers. She may have controlled them coming together in her house, but now, he was going to take the reins.

It may have been a while for him, but it was like riding a bike.

He broke the kiss and ghosted his lips along her flesh, needing to taste all of her. He arrived at her mounds and didn't hesitate capturing one with his mouth. He teased her nipple with his tongue, massaging and squeezing the other with his free hand.

"Stan," she breathed.

Her fingers were in his hair, driving him crazy. He loved the sound of his name on her lips and couldn't wait to hear her shout it aloud.

His tongue burned a path over to her other breast. He took his time in tasting it, bathing her nipple, then continued his journey south. Her legs widened to allow him to settle between them. He nudged them open farther, taking in her center.

His pulse quickened at the sight of her brown slit, already slick with her desire. Her swollen clit peeking out from between her two labia. He breathed in her scent and loved it. He gently laid kisses along her thigh, teasing her.

Nasia writhed on the floor, calling his name. She tried to guide his head to her, but he resisted. Having a woman who knew what she wanted and wasn't afraid to show it was a complete turn-on.

He brushed his lips against her thighs, making his way back to his final destination. Spreading her labia open, he slid his tongue through her slit, taking his first taste of her.

She was just as sweet as he knew she would be.

Stan latched on to her clit, her body jerking

underneath his touch. The sexiest noises escaped her as he sucked it. Her hips moved in a slow rhythm, bringing her pussy farther into his mouth. He flicked her little bean and introduced one finger into her slick core.

"God, yes," she moaned.

He bit back a chuckle, swiveling his finger inside her. Sliding another one in, he wanted to stretch her out to prepare her for him. She was a small woman, and he was a big man. He needed to ensure he didn't hurt her. Her pussy was already drenched, and there wouldn't be a problem in that department.

He slowly thrust his fingers inside, setting a steady rhythm, and continued to focus on her clit.

Nasia grew louder, her hips bucking toward him. He curved his fingers upwards, stroking the top of her vaginal wall. He increased the pull on her clit, the combination proving to be too much for her.

Nasia's body tensed, her back arching from the floor as her climax washed over her. His name was on her lips when she yelled, her fingers gripped his hair painfully, but it was well worth it. She could snatch him bald for all he cared, just so he could hear her call his name again.

She flopped down, her breaths coming fast, her

eyes closed. Climbing over her, he grinned looking at her flushed face.

The old boy still has it.

He gripped the base of his cock to steady it. He ran it through her slit, a grunt escaping him at the sensation of her honey coating him. He lined up the blunt tip of his shaft at her entrance.

Her eyes opened and met his gaze while he pushed into her. A groan vibrated from the depths of his soul at the feeling of her silky channel enveloping him.

A shudder racked his body.

She was so fucking tight.

"Ahh," he moaned, unable to hold it in. He paused, wanting to sink into her slowly.

"It's all right. I can take it," Nasia whispered in between pants.

She lifted her leg and pulled him to her, and he sank completely inside her. She was so wet, he couldn't think of anything else but the feeling of her wrapped around him.

"Nasia." Her name tore from his lips. His self-control was hanging by a thread. He bent down and crushed his lips to hers.

Nasia kissed him back, her tongue inviting his in. The kiss grew deeper, and her nails dug into his back. There was a desperate need burning inside him.

He drew his hips back then plunged deep again, setting a steady rhythm. He couldn't get close enough to her, nor deep enough inside.

"Yes," she hissed, her nails scraping down his back.

Her breathless cries fueled him on. He brought her leg up to rest on his shoulder. The change in position sent a jolt of electricity straight to his balls. He could feel every tremor in her body and her muscles clenching around him.

Closing his eyes tight, he would have sworn he saw stars. Everything was so right between them.

"Harder," she moaned.

The last piece of control he had was ripped away from him.

His hips jackhammered his cock into her, unable to control his pace.

Nasia's cries carried through the air along with his. He was lost in the woman beneath him and couldn't think of anything else but Nasia.

Nothing else mattered.

His eyes fluttered open, and his gaze landing on the sight of his cock thrusting in and out of her slick channel had a growl ripping from his throat.

It was the perfect sight. She may be small, but Nasia took every inch of him without complaint.

A possessiveness took over him. He wanted to watch her fall apart on his cock like she had on his tongue.

Nasia's eyes opened, their gazes connecting.

The familiar sensation of an electrical current starting in the base of his balls shot through him.

His climax was near.

Sliding a hand between them, he strummed her clit.

"Stan." Nasia's eyes rolled back, her body arching toward his.

Her nails once again dug into his skin, but he ignored the sharp pain. Her head flew back, her mouth opened with a scream tearing from her.

Her muscles clamped down around his cock, taking the last bit of breath from his body.

Stan's hips pumped furiously, his orgasm rocking him. He roared, emptying himself into her.

Nasia gripped his shoulder, his body practically falling on top of her. His heart hammered as he released her leg.

Stan braced himself on his elbows to keep from crushing her. He outweighed her by at least sixty pounds. He rested his forehead on hers, their breathing still coming rapidly.

Her hands skated along his shoulders and came to his jaw. He opened his eyes and met her gaze. A small smile played on her lips. She guided him down to her, taking his lips in a slow, deep, passionate kiss.

"Will you stay the night with me?" she asked softly, studying him.

She wiggled slightly under him. His semisoft cock was a still buried in her, and her movements were jerking him back to attention.

"I thought you'd never ask." He lowered his head again and claimed her lips.

❧ 6 ❧

Nasia tried to roll over, but something was keeping her from moving. She opened her eyes and found a hand resting on her naked belly.

Stan.

She grinned, loving the feeling of his muscular body spooning hers. Her body still tingled from the lovemaking they had shared. She turned over to face him. She nuzzled her face into the crook of his neck.

He enveloped her, bringing her flush against him. He adjusted the blankets around them. She smiled. He was such a sweetheart, a gentleman, and a freaking sex god.

The man certainly knew his way around a

woman's body. Her throat was a little scratchy from her screaming practically the entire night.

She was one lucky woman.

She breathed in his scent. It was woodsy, almost earthy in nature, and if she had to bottle the scent of a man, it would be Stan.

"Morning," his deep voice rumbled. His hand slid along the curve of her back in slow, steady strokes, coming to rest on the curve of her ass.

"Morning to you." Her fingers danced along his abdomen. She had taken her time to count every ridge with her tongue. They had gotten to know each other very intimately.

Nasia didn't hold any regrets in her heart for sleeping—having sex with him; there was barely any sleeping. It was the day of the modern woman, he was good friends with someone she trusted, who vouched for him, and it had ended with a night of explosive sex.

Her fingers slowly traveled down his stomach. It trembled from his laughter spilling from him. His free hand rested on hers, holding it in place.

"You're playing a dangerous game, woman." He kissed the top of her head.

"What game? I'm just wanting to say good morning to him, too. I don't want him to feel neglected," she joked. She broke free from his hold and continued on to her destination. Nasia wrapped it around the base of his shaft, finding him growing rigid.

"He's not." Stan's quick intake of breath could be heard.

She stroked the length of his long shaft, her core clenching, remembering the sensation of him sinking inside her.

Pushing up on her elbow, she continued, watching Stan's face. His eyes were closed, and his expression was that of someone experiencing pure ecstasy.

Nasia's heart raced. She loved that she had given this man so much pleasure through the night.

His blue eyes fluttered open and met her gaze.

"We can't stay in bed all day." He reached underneath the blanket, stilling hers.

"Really?" Her eyebrows rose high. "Are you sure?"

"We have to eat sometime," he murmured. He brought her hand to his lips and kissed the back of it. He cupped her cheek and covered her lips. "If I recall, I asked to take you out and you accepted."

"I did, but there is so much more we can do here," she assured him.

She let out a shriek when he suddenly moved, rolling them over until he was braced above her. He settled between her legs, and she groaned from the feeling of his hardened member resting near her core.

"I'm sure there is, and we will come back to that." He laughed.

Nasia saw how relaxed he appeared. She knew she would know what he needed now, if only she could get him to follow her advice.

"But—"

"No buts." He dropped a kiss on her lips.

She skated her hand up to the nape of his neck in an attempt to hold him in place, but he was too fast. He snagged her wrists and pinned them down over her head. His gaze dropped down to her breasts thrusting toward him.

Leaning down, he nipped one of her nipples, moving off the bed. "You are a temptation I'm going to have to avoid."

She chuckled and turned on her side, bracing her head on her hand as she watched him stride across the room. Nasia bit her lip to keep from groaning aloud. His body was chiseled, firm muscles everywhere, and she had spent plenty of time exploring them with her tongue.

"Are you sure we have to eat?" She pouted.

"Yes. I'm a man of my word, and we're going to go out to eat. Now let's shower." He snagged her foot and dragged her to the edge of the bed.

A scream escaped her when his hand brushed against the arch of her foot. She was extremely ticklish and tried to get away from him.

His laughter filled the air, and she thrashed around the bed, unable to breathe due to laughing hysterically.

"Now, that's something I'm going to have to keep in the back of my mind." He pulled her from the bed, her body leaning into his.

She rested her head on his chest, trying to control her breathing.

"Are we going to have to swing by your house for fresh clothes?" she asked once she was able to drag air into her lungs normally.

"Nah, I keep a bag in my truck." Stan shook his head. "Sometimes I crash at the ranch during the busy seasons. Go ahead and get the water ready. I'll be right back."

He dropped another kiss on her lips. She nodded and stepped away from him, heading into the bathroom. Excitement filled her at the thought of spending the entire day with him. He was a great guy, and she was definitely going to ensure they explored this. Last night would not be a one-night stand.

Stan was in for a surprise.

He now had a girlfriend.

Nasia glanced at herself in the mirror and barked a laugh. She looked like someone who had spent the entire night getting her back blown out. Her hair stood up everywhere, and a silly grin was ingrained on her face.

Her stomach chose that moment to growl.

"Okay, maybe the man had a point," she grumbled. Reaching for her brush, she quickly got all the kinks out of her hair and wrapped it, covering her head with her silk scarf.

Nasia started the shower and let the water run. By the time the steam started filling the room, the door to the bathroom opened with Stan entering.

"You're just in time." She spun around and grabbed her shower cap to cover her head. There was no way in hell she was risking getting her head wet today. Her appointment with Yani wasn't until next week, and she didn't want to have to wrestle with her hair on her own.

Stan moved over to the shower and stuck his hand in. "What the devil!"

"What?" Her eyes widened as he adjusted the temperature.

"I'm not trying to be boiled alive, woman," he muttered. Once he felt it was appropriate, he got in.

"Aw, afraid of a little warm water?" She followed him in. Nasia froze in place watching him lean back in the water, allowing it to flow onto his head. Her gaze tracked the trail of water sliding down his body.

Swallowing hard, she blinked.

"Only when it's hot enough to take off the first layer of my skin." He grinned at her, and her heart stuttered.

Jesus, how could this man be so sexy?

And he was currently all hers.

Nasia stepped to him, unable to resist touching him. Her hands explored his chest and the ridges of his abdomen. His quick intake of breath was barely heard over the running water.

"Nasia," he groaned. He brought her flush to him, covering her mouth with his.

Nasia ignored the chilled wall when her back hit it. Stan covered her front with his body, and that's all she could comprehend.

She needed him.

Again.

STAN OPENED THE DOOR TO THE TIPSY COW and ushered Nasia inside. It was a local bar and restaurant all of the locals frequented on the weekend.

"Have you been here yet since you've been back?" he asked Nasia. He kept his hand on the small of her back.

"No, not yet. I've heard good things about this place." Nasia turned her big brown eyes on him.

His gaze dropped down to a darkened area on her neck. Flashbacks came to mind. That was his mark he'd put on her. He just couldn't get enough of her. Seeing her marked by him did strange things to him.

"They have great food, and their lunch specials are the best."

He had planned to take her out for breakfast, but once she'd run her hands along him, all thoughts of food had gone out the window.

Three hours later, here they were.

An early lunch.

There was a good lunch rush.

"Hey, Stan," Sonya greeted him. She came over to them with a wide smile on her face. "Just two of you?"

"Yup."

"Give us about five minutes or so. One of the busboys called in sick, so I'm cleaning tables, too," Sonya said.

"That's fine. No rush." Stan pushed his hat back on his head and looked around. Pretty much all the tables were full. They moved away from the door and stood near the bar so people could leave without them in the way.

"I'm famished." Nasia patted her belly. "Wonder why?"

"Seriously?" he scoffed. His little sex kitten was insatiable. It had been years since he had spent so much time in bed making love to a beautiful woman.

Hell, the last time was when he and Victoria—

Stan immediately put a halt to the train of thought quick. His ex-wife was not going to creep up into his thoughts while he was out with Nasia. She was in the past and was going to stay there.

He brought his arm up to rest on Nasia's shoulders and pulled her in close to him. He was a lucky man. She was beautiful, smart, had a sense of humor that matched his, and was a woman who knew what she wanted sexually.

When they had finally dressed, she had poured herself into skintight jeans, a white graphic t-shirt with a woman with an Afro on it, and she paired it with multicolored heels. Her makeup was light, and her dark hair rested on her shoulders.

He wasn't sure what she had done to it, but once she took the scarf off her head, it fell perfectly.

"Do you come here often?" Nasia leaned into him.

"Yeah. Usually with the Brooks brothers on the weekends once in a while. Now they are all getting married, it's usually me, Carson, Karl, and Darnell." He dropped a kiss to her forehead.

"So, they are all getting hitched so they can't come out to play as often?" She laughed.

"Something like that." He chuckled.

Parker had his hands full with his new wife, a baby, and their rambunctious son, Tyler. Wade was engaged to Joy, they were expecting, and now Rashad was with Yani. His little circle of single buddies was getting smaller every time he turned around. Going out with the guys had helped him stay sane after the divorce. They were all there for him.

The Brooks brothers and his friends made sure he

never had to drink alone to drown his sorrows. Parker, Wade, and Carson ensured he had plenty of work to keep him busy.

He appreciated everything they had done for him.

They were good men.

His gaze dropped down to Nasia, and he wondered, would this turn into something more? Or was this just a fun weekend fling?

"What are you staring at?" He tweaked her nose.

"That woman staring at us from the bar." She nodded toward someone behind him.

He glanced over his shoulder and froze.

Victoria was sitting at the bar with her friend, Leslie. He hadn't seen her in months. She hadn't moved from Shady Springs but had got a place on the outskirts of town. He wasn't even sure if her and Connor were still together. He hadn't wanted to speak to either of them since the divorce. After the signing of the papers at the magistrate's office, he'd walked out and hadn't looked back.

"Is that, um, her?" Nasia whispered.

He turned back to her and jerked his head in a nod.

"Do you still feel anything for her?" she asked softly.

"Hell, no." It was a knee-jerk reaction. Stan

believed in truth and honesty. He wouldn't lie to Nasia.

What he had once felt for Victoria was gone.

"Stan?" a soft voice sounded behind him.

He closed his eyes for a moment, unable to believe she would come over to them.

Where was Sonya? Wasn't the table ready yet?

Victoria came to stand before him and Nasia. Curiosity was burning in her eyes as her gaze landed on Nasia.

Nasia leaned more into him and wrapped a possessive arm around his waist.

"Victoria." He nodded, keeping his greeting short and curt. With everything they had been through, she was lucky he was even acknowledging her.

"You look good." She tucked her blonde hair behind her ear. "Who's your friend?"

Stan opened his mouth to tell her none of her business, but Nasia beat him to the punch.

"Hi, I'm Nasia, Stan's girlfriend. You must be Victoria," Nasia replied haughtily. She tilted her head to the side and studied Victoria.

Stan tried to see his ex-wife as Nasia would.

They were about the same height, but that was where the similarities stopped. Victoria was thin, blonde, with huge green eyes. She was a selfish woman, he'd realized after they had divorced. Everything in their relationship had been about her. Where they ate, what movies they watched, where they traveled…he was just expected to pay.

Which he hadn't had a problem with. He was raised to be a provider, but nothing he ever did was good enough for her.

"Yes, I am. Stan talks about me?" A small smile spread on her face. The narcissist in her would love to hear he'd been talking about her.

"Not a word. I just put two and two together." Nasia shook her head.

"Oh." Victoria stood tall, her eyes narrowing on Nasia prior to latching her attention back on him. "I didn't know you had started seeing anyone."

"Why would you? It's none of your business." He shrugged and looked away.

"Well, with as much as you work, when would you have time?" Victoria rolled her eyes.

"Oh, he makes time for me." Nasia ran her hand along his chest.

He glanced down into her big brown eyes and felt a stirring beneath his belt.

She broke their stare and set her sights on Victoria. "I make it very worth it. I have no problems holding his attention."

Stan had to hold back the laughter threatening to spill from him.

Victoria sputtered, her face growing flushed. "Listen here, my husband—"

"Ex-husband," Nasia interjected.

Stan felt her body grow tense, and as much as he would love to see Nasia scratch Victoria's eyes out, he couldn't allow that. At least not on their first date.

"You made sure of that, so don't go forgetting it now, honey. He's with me." Nasia's voice dripped venom, turning him on and pissing Victoria off.

Stan loved it.

"Hey, Stan. Your table is ready." Sonya came over with a haggard expression on her face.

"Wait a minute—"

"We would love to chat, but my man needs to feed me." Nasia took his hand and practically dragged him behind her.

At the moment, he would follow this woman anywhere.

Sonya stopped at an available booth in the back and motioned for them to sit.

"I'm sorry about the wait," she began, but he waved her off.

"Not a problem," Stan said.

She set menus down for them and took their drink orders and disappeared.

He sat back in the booth and took in Nasia who was glancing over the menu. She was calm and collected as if she hadn't just confronted his ex.

Nasia Henry was one hell of a woman.

"What's good here?" she asked, not looking up.

"Girlfriend, huh?" He took off his Stetson and rested it on the hook at the edge of the booth. He ignored Victoria's stare from across the restaurant and turned his attention back to the amazing woman sitting opposite him.

She grinned and met his gaze.

"You think after the night and morning we had, that I was letting you walk out of my house unclaimed?" Her perfectly sculpted eyebrows rose high.

He barked a hefty laugh, unsure when the last time was where he had laughed so much. Tears blurred his vision from her attempt at innocence with her proclamation. He wiped his face and shook his head.

"Come here, woman." He leaned over and grabbed her hand.

She slid around the table and went straight under his arm.

He held her close and tipped her chin up. "Well, since we are making this relationship official between us, I think we need to seal it with a kiss."

Nasia's smile grew brighter.

He leaned down and touched his lips to hers.

❄ 7 ❄

"Hey, boss. Your cowboy is here," Sara called out from the door. She had a wide grin and wiggled her eyebrows.

Nasia glanced up from the concoction she was making. She had debuted her new muffin, and it sold out every day. From the response of the town, she may have to make it a regular item on the menu.

Now she had to find something to top it for next month.

For the past three weeks, she and Stan had been inseparable. Every morning before he went to the ranch, he stopped by the café to get his coffee and breakfast.

She looked forward to their morning coffee together.

Nasia arrived every morning around four to prep and begin baking for the day. Sara was one of her trusted employees who came in early also to help.

"Thanks." Nasia wiped her hands on her apron then removed it. She glanced down at the counter and just left everything where it was. She had made a mess of things. Since she was doing strawberry this month, she wanted to make something chocolatey. She had a mind to make a s'mores breakfast muffin and was trying to get the combo of chocolate and marshmallows right.

"So, are you two an item?" Sara asked.

"Yes, ma'am." Nasia breezed past Sara and headed out to the café. After breakfast with Stan, she'd go back into the kitchen to finish her experiment.

Her gaze landed on her big, handsome cowboy standing in line staring at the menu. She rolled her eyes and headed behind the counter to make their coffee.

He had to have tried everything on the menu by now.

"Stan," she called out.

He turned those bright-blue eyes to her, and her heart skipped a beat.

She waved him over to where she stood. "You know you don't have to get in line."

"Well, I was checking to see if you changed anything on the menu." He gave her his killer-watt smile, and her panties just about went up in flames.

"You know anything I add, you automatically get to taste." He loved when she brought things to his place for him to try out. He was like her own personal taste tester.

Each day he worked, he stopped by the café first. Even on his off days he still stopped in. The past few weeks had been wonderful.

The nights even better.

"All right then. You choose what I'm eating then," he said. He leaned against the counter and tossed her a wink. "I trust you."

"Go have a seat. I'll fix you up something up nice, darlin'," she drawled in a poor Southern accent.

Within minutes she had two tall coffees doctored to their liking and two warmed strawberry shortcake muffins. Placing them on a tray, she carried them over to where Stan was seated. She took the chair next to him and sat the tray down in the middle of the table.

"God, I've missed you." Stan rested his forearm on the back of her chair. He leaned over and nuzzled her neck. He snuck in and pressed a hot, open-mouthed kiss on her skin.

Her body trembled with need. If only they weren't in her place of business...

"Don't tease me," she murmured.

"Not teasing. Just giving you a heads-up for what is going to come later." He chuckled. He pulled back and reached for his coffee.

"Is that so, cowboy?"

"Hmm...don't fret, Nasia. I'm a man of my word." He winked at her.

"Oh, cowboy, take me away," she dramatically gasped. She held the back of her hand to her forehead, fluttering her eyelashes seductively.

His grin widened at her silliness. "I plan to."

"What time are you getting off?" She skillfully changed the subject. Otherwise, she might drag him off to her office and make him late for work. She was quickly learning ranch hands worked long hours daily, and she respected it.

Someone had to do it.

Stan loved his job and the family he worked for.

Who was she to stand in the way? She, too, worked long hours at the café. It was her baby and her responsibility, and all of her hard work was paying off.

Soon, she'd be able to hire more employees and maybe even an assistant manager to help run things, so she didn't have to come before the crack of dawn every day.

"Well, I plan to get off at four, go home and shower, and then surprise my girlfriend with a night out with some friends." Stan took a sip of his coffee.

"Is that so?" Nasia exclaimed dramatically. She grabbed her muffin, tearing it in half, then took a bite of it.

Stan reached forward and stole the other half and popped it in his mouth.

"Hey! Eat your own."

"Yours tastes better." He grinned, reaching for his.

Nasia really didn't care. Stan was going to be leaving to go work on a ranch, he could have both if he wanted. He would need the calories. The man could pack away some food. If Nasia ate half of what he did, her hips would be four times wider than they already were.

"So, what do you have in mind?" she asked, already thinking of what she could wear.

"Wade, Joy, Yani, and Rashad are getting together to go bowling. Rashad invited us to come along."

"I haven't been bowling in years. I'm game."

Nasia sipped her coffee. She really enjoyed their time together in the morning. It never lasted long, but she cherished every minute. They were getting to know each other, and she loved spending time with him.

"Good." He popped the rest of his muffin in his mouth. He glanced down at his watch and released a curse. "I have to go, babe."

"Okay." She tried not to pout, but she knew he couldn't spend all morning together. That didn't mean she didn't miss him while he was gone. They stood from the table. "Don't worry about the trash, I'll come back and get it. What time should I be ready?"

"About six." Stan snagged his coffee and took her hand in his, entwining their fingers together.

She ignored Sara's silly grin and wink as they passed the counter. They walked out the restaurant and headed over to Stan's pickup truck. He opened the door and set his coffee down inside the cup holder on the console.

Nasia waited for him to turn around. He shut the door, rested back against the vehicle, and pulled her to him.

"I will make sure I am ready by six," she announced.

Nasia wrapped her arms around him and leaned into his hardened body.

"See that you are." His hands skated down to the swell of her ass and held her in place against him.

Nasia bit back a moan at the sensation of his bulge pressing into her stomach. He tilted her chin up, pressing a kiss to her lips. She opened her mouth and allowed his tongue to sweep inside. His tongue stroked hers, eliciting a moan from her.

Her pulse pounded as the kiss deepened. She fisted his shirt, holding her steady to keep her knees from giving out.

A horn blared off in the distance. They jerked apart and stared at each other.

"Think of me while you're at work?" She smoothed out his shirt and stepped back.

"Always."

STAN WALKED THROUGH HIS HOUSE, FRESH from his shower. A towel was wrapped around his waist as he made his way to the kitchen. He was suddenly parched. He used another towel to dry his hair.

Work had flown by, and he was anxious to get

over to Nasia's. He loved spending time with her. He had gotten to know everything about her and her family. She was extremely close with her sister and parents.

Nasia was understanding of the long hours he worked. She never made him feel guilty. Hell, the woman was a workaholic, too. She had to be to ensure her business survived, and he understood. She always made sure he was taken care of by feeding him the minute he stepped foot into her home. He had a big appetite, and the woman sure knew her way around the kitchen and the bedroom.

Things were never boring between the two of them.

A grin lingered on his lips. He had half a mind to skip going out for bowling and just locking himself in his bedroom with Nasia and throwing away the key.

He'd loved diving between those smooth brown thighs of his woman.

Entering the kitchen, he headed straight to the fridge, tossing the small towel on his shoulder. He pulled out a bottle of water from the fridge. He removed the top and took a long sip.

The doorbell sounded.

"Who the hell is that?" he muttered.

It had better not be Nasia. She had teased him that she would just meet him at his place. It wouldn't make sense since her place was on the way to the bowling alley.

He finished off the water and tossed the bottle away. Towel secured, he went to the front door.

"Shit."

The front door had three large windowpanes that allowed him to see who was standing on the other side.

Victoria.

What the hell is she doing here?

He would have ignored the doorbell, but she turned around and spotted him in the foyer. He marched over and opened the door.

"What do you want?" he asked.

Victoria froze in place and stared at him. Her gaze roamed his chest and jumped back up to meet his eyes. Her hand toyed with the collar of her button-down shirt.

"May I come in?" she asked.

"For what?" He kept his hand on the handle, not wanting to budge.

"We need to talk." Her eyes widened in the facial expression that used to fool him every time when she wanted something.

"There's nothing we have to say. Everything between us was worked out down at the magistrate's office with the divorce settlement."

"Stan, please. I promise this won't take long."

He brushed a hand along his face and blew out a deep breath. He didn't have time for this shit.

"Fine. Five minutes." He opened the door wider to allow her room to step into his home.

Victoria moved forward and stepped into the foyer. Stan shut the door and walked into the living room with her behind him.

"So what is it you want to talk about?" He folded his arms in front of his chest and glared at her.

"Your place looks nice. Simple, but nice," she said, turning in a circle.

When they had moved into their home when they'd first relocated to Shady Springs, Victoria had picked everything out for the house. At the time he hadn't cared since he was just starting work at the Blazing Eagle Ranch. It appeared to make her happy, so he'd let her pick out everything. The only things he required was a big enough bed to sleep in, a couch, a huge television to watch football, and a fridge.

He was simple man.

"I'm sure you didn't come over here to give me decorating suggestions."

"No, I didn't." She rotated around and didn't say anything for a moment. She appeared nervous, and it piqued his curiosity. "Are you doing well?"

A snort escaped him. "I'm doing fan-fucking-tabulous."

"You look really good, Stan," she whispered. Her hand trembled as she reached up to tuck her thick blonde hair behind her ear. "Have you been working out? You seem bigger…more muscular."

Her gaze appeared stuck on his chest. Maybe he should go put some clothes on. Years ago, he would have loved to have her gaze at him the way hers was.

Now, it only made him want to cover himself up.

"What do you want, Victoria?" he snapped.

She needed to get to the point or leave.

He would prefer the latter.

He didn't want to be late picking Nasia up.

"Do you ever think of us?" she asked.

What the fuck?

"Excuse me?" He couldn't be hearing her right. Did he think of them? He sure did—when they were married and before he found out she was spreading her legs for Connor.

"Do you ever think about us?" she repeated.

"No." He shook his head. It had taken a while, but eventually he had stopped harping on about what had gone wrong with their relationship, and he had become numb.

But then he met a gorgeous café owner who turned his entire world around on its axis in just a short amount of time.

He was completely infatuated with Nasia.

"I see." She fidgeted with her hands and shuffled her feet slightly. "Stan, I made a big mistake. I came over there to tell you that I'm sorry for being so selfish and for hurting you. I don't know what came over me and I'm here asking for you to give me another chance."

Stan froze in place, unable to believe the words she'd said.

"You and Connor—"

"Aren't together anymore. We broke up about two months after our divorce was finalized." She stood to her full height with a glint of determination in her eyes.

Well, ain't that some shit.

He had met Connor their freshman year in college. They had been assigned as roommates and had hit it off well. Connor was a manwhore. Always had been and always would be. Hell, he had been

Stan's best man at their wedding.

He just hadn't realized Connor would stoop so low as to sleep with Victoria.

Stan hadn't wanted to hear the explanations from either of them.

Victoria's excuse was she wasn't getting attention from him, but whenever Connor came to visit, she felt like a new woman.

Connor's excuse?

Victoria came on to him.

She had risked her marriage for a relationship that was set up to fail from the start. Connor wasn't a settling type of guy. Even at their age, he changed his women as much as Stan changed socks.

Stan didn't trust any of the words coming out of her mouth at the moment. She had broken the bond between them the minute she'd slid into bed with his best friend.

"I'm sorry to hear, but I've moved on."

"With the woman from the bar." She sighed. Her face scrunched up, her head shaking side to side. "She just doesn't seem like your type."

"What is that supposed to mean?" He narrowed his gaze on her.

"She doesn't look like the type of woman you

would date." Victoria shrugged. "She's very outspoken, has an attitude, and she just don't look like—"

"Watch it, Victoria," he snarled. He was two seconds from tossing her out of his home. The matter of skin color had never been discussed between him or Nasia. It just didn't matter. He liked her for who she was and the same for her.

He never knew Victoria to be racist, but he wouldn't be surprised. She had grown up in a secluded high-middle-class family, and the amount of minorities in Shady Springs was low.

Not that it was an excuse.

At one point, he had thought he knew Victoria and she wouldn't have been the cheating type.

"I'm not saying it as a bad thing. I'm not racist, I have black friends." She shrugged again.

"You know that is something racist people say, right?" He cocked an eyebrow high. This was un-fucking-believable. "And your one black 'friend' you have was your coworker, Tamika, who you don't even hang out with outside of work, so if anything, she would be considered a work acquaintance."

Her cheeks flushed red.

"I don't want to argue with you, all I was saying is that you've never been with a black woman, and I just don't understand why now." She rested her hands on her waist.

Couldn't she hear what she sounded like?

"Well, first of all, she's not a selfish bitch who I can't trust," he began.

Victoria flinched but remained quiet.

"She's understanding about my work, she's supportive, and she makes me laugh." There was much more about Nasia, but it was none of Victoria's business.

"But it's not serous, is it? I mean, we were together for so long, don't you want to try to give us another chance?" she pleaded. "We were good together."

She moved toward him, but he backed away with his hands held up in the air. His skin crawled with just the thought of her hands touching his bare skin.

"You need to go," he said. He smoothed a hand through his hair and ensured the towel was secured around his waist.

This conversation was over.

Stan stalked to the front door and opened it. Victoria followed behind him, stopping inches from him in the doorway.

"Can you just think about it?" she asked.

"Goodbye, Victoria." He landed his level gaze on

her and waited for her to clear the door so he could close it.

She studied his eyes, jerking her head in a nod, then marched out of the house. Stan shut the door and flipped the lock. He strode back into his bedroom and sat on the edge of his bed.

What the hell was that? He leaned his head into his hands and blew out a deep breath.

Had she asked for his forgiveness after he had caught her with Connor, he might have reconsidered it.

Why after all of this time?

Now, after he'd had time to process everything and met Nasia, there was no way he would ever consider taking her back.

She was in the past and was going to stay there.

His future was looking really bright at the moment, and it included a curvy brown-skinned beauty with a perfect smile that made his heart race.

❧ 8 ❧

"No, no, no!" Nasia shouted. She stood braced, watching her bowling ball curve toward the gutter. "Go right!"

She danced along as if she could magically straighten out her ball as it sailed down the lane. It managed to stay on the slippery wooden floor and knock down three pins.

"That's all right," Yani shouted.

Nasia spun around and laughed. They were having a great time and were on their second game. They had paired off, girls versus the guys.

The guys had won the first one, and they were not ashamed to keep throwing it in the girls' faces.

Nasia's gaze landed on Stan who sat quiet. He smiled and joked around, but she knew something was bothering him. From the moment she'd opened the door when he'd arrived to pick her up, she noticed he seemed a little distanced, lost in his thoughts.

She had asked him what was wrong, but he'd shaken his head and smiled, but it hadn't reached his eyes.

"Let me show you how to do it," Rashad teased, picking up his ball.

She stuck her tongue out at him and made her way to her seat. They had ordered food and drinks, enjoying each other's company.

Nasia hadn't known Joy before tonight, but she was a real sweetheart, funny, very competitive when it came to bowling. Her family owned the sheep farm that bordered the Brooks' cattle ranch.

Rashad walked up to the line, allowing the woman in the next lane to take her turn.

Nasia, Yani, and Joy leaned forward, waiting for the right moment.

"Babe, this is how you're supposed to bowl." Rashad looked over his shoulder at Yani.

"Whatever. Throw the damn ball already," Yani replied.

He began walking forward, and that was their cue.

"Gutter! Gutter! Gutter!" they chanted simultaneously amongst a fit of giggles.

He tossed his ball and sent it flying down the lane.

Seven pins went down.

"Damn, I just knew that would work." Yani snorted.

"You girls think you're funny. I'm going to clean up this spare." Rashad wagged a finger at them.

Nasia sat back and grabbed her Coke. She turned her attention to Stan who was staring at her. She winked at him, eliciting a smile from him.

Her heart skipped a beat at the sexy grin.

"Anyone want anything from the bar?" Wade asked, standing and stretching.

"I'll take another Sprite." Joy held up her empty glass. She rubbed her pregnant belly and grinned.

"I'll go with you." Stan pushed up from his seat. He turned to Nasia. "Want anything?"

She hadn't had an alcoholic drink all night. One wouldn't hurt.

"Yeah, cranberry and vodka, please," Nasia replied.

"I'll have the same as her," Yani said.

The guys left, heading over to the bar.

"So how long have you and Stan been an item?"

Joy settled back on the cushioned bench. Her hand unconsciously landed on her belly as she watched Nasia.

"About a month." Nasia smiled. It had been a great month and seemed longer.

"He's a great guy. When I first met him, he was really quiet. You two look good together." Joy nodded.

"Don't they?" Yani chuckled. "The second Nasia started asking about him, I knew I had to help my girl out."

Nasia rolled her eyes. Of course, Yani would take the credit for getting her and Stan together.

"What about you and Wade?" Nasia asked.

The two looked as if they had been together forever.

"Not too long. I've known him practically my entire life since we grew up next door to each other." Joy was a pretty girl, and when she smiled, Nasia could see why Wade was captivated by her. "I heard you're the owner of the Shady Bean Café. I'm going to have to come check you out."

"Please do." Nasia enjoyed talking about her business to anyone who would listen.

They continued chatting about their line of work with Joy setting up an appointment with Yani to Joy inviting Nasia on her farm to see if they could do business. Nasia loved using fresh ingredients and had already made connections with other local farmers.

"What are you women chatting about so enthusiastically?" Wade asked.

The guys returned with drinks in hand.

The girls made room for them. Stan took his seat by Nasia and handed her a glass. He had gotten a long-neck beer bottle for himself. She recognized that he pretty much drank one kind and made a mental note to pick some up next time she went to the grocery store.

"Thanks," she murmured.

He rested his arm along the back of the booth. Nasia scooted closer, loving the feeling of him against her.

"Girl stuff," Joy replied haughtily.

"None of ya business," Yani teased.

"Well, damn. Guess we aren't needed, fellas," Rashad joked.

"Hush up." Yani elbowed him.

Rashad fell back as if she had really injured him. Chuckles went around.

"Don't let her get away with that, Rashad. I

believed that's domestic abuse. Stan and I are witnesses." Wade laughed.

"Hear, hear." Stan tipped his bottle to Rashad.

"Hey." Nasia reached down and pinched Stan's side. The man barely had any fat on his body. She was so jealous; her tummy was nice and soft.

"What?" Stan jerked away from her playfully. "We men have to stick together."

"Well, I hope you men know how to keep yourself warm at night," Joy teased.

"On second thought. I didn't see anything," Stan claimed. He leaned over and dropped a kiss on Nasia's forehead.

Nasia laughed. This had been a good idea. It helped her get to meet another woman who she wouldn't mind getting to know and calling a friend. With the move and getting her business off the ground, it left little time to actually go out and meet people. She had been away from Shady Springs so long, it was like she was brand-new to the town.

Instead of finishing the game, they sat around talking and laughing. Stories from the ranch had Nasia with tears streaming down her face.

"We'll have to do this again," Joy said.

"Yeah, maybe one night we can talk Parker and

Maddy into getting a babysitter and joining us," Wade suggested.

"That would be great. That woman needs to get away." Yani chuckled.

"I'm down. Just let us know," Stan said.

Nasia was having a hard time concentrating with his fingers playing with her hair.

He glanced down at her. "Ready to go?"

Nasia nodded.

They stood and said their goodbyes.

Once in the truck, Nasia turned to face Stan. She took the time to study him. He guided the vehicle onto the street. They rode in silence for a minute, but Nasia just had to ask.

"Seriously. What is wrong?" she asked softly.

He looked at her, and again, she could see the distance in his eyes. She reached for his hand and brought it to her lips.

She kissed the back of it, entwining their fingers together. "Just tell me."

He tightened his grip on her and blew out a deep breath.

Worry settled in, but she tried to not let it consume her, but his first words just about sent her into cardiac arrest.

"Victoria stopped by my house today."

AS MUCH AS HE TRIED TO NOT LET IT bother him, Victoria's visit had left a sour taste in his mouth. He'd tried to push it down all night, but it kept popping up in his mind.

Nasia had immediately picked up on it, and he attempted to act as if nothing was wrong.

He hated sharing anything about his painful past with her. He didn't want to be a burden on issues that happened before she came into his life.

"Okay," she murmured.

He tightened the grip on her hand, disliking the tremor he detected in her voice. She had absolutely nothing to worry about.

That chapter of his life was closed, and he was not returning to it.

"I didn't want to bring it up." He grimaced, not wanting to spoil their date, but he was an honest man and would be like an open book with Nasia. That was something he'd taken away from his failed marriage. They had to be truthful with each other. Had Victoria come to him with her complaints about him and their marriage before she'd cheated, there was a slight chance they may still be married.

"What did she want?"

"She came to apologize for wrecking our marriage." He snorted. He braked at a red light, flipping his blinker on. He faced Nasia, wanting to look her in the eye. "Nothing happened. I didn't let her stay long. She said her piece, then I made her leave."

"Why would she come by for that?"

"I have no clue." He shook his head, running a trembling hand through his hair. That was the million-dollar question. Was it because she had seen him out with Nasia and got jealous, or was she truly wanting to right her wrong so they could try again?

"What happened between the two of you? I know she cheated, but was that the only issue?"

The light changed to green. He pushed his foot down on the gas and turned on the main road that led to Nasia's home.

"Honestly, I couldn't even begin to tell you. One moment I thought everything was good between the two of us, but apparently it wasn't. She said I worked too much, never spent time with her, she felt abandoned. Am I perfect? No, but I worked my ass off to provide a great home, ensure we were financially stable, and what did she go and do? Slept with my fucking friend who told her she was pretty."

It felt good to say that aloud. It was like a weight off his shoulders. He hadn't really shared it with many people. He glanced over at Nasia expecting to see pity, but it wasn't there.

"I don't mean to unload all of this on you." He sighed.

"Don't worry. I asked, remember?" she said.

Her other hand came to rest on top of their collapsed hands, and for some reason, it comforted him.

He pulled into her driveway, leaving the engine idling.

"I appreciate you." He leaned his head back on the headrest and stared at her.

"Why don't you come in?" she asked, a small smile playing on her lips.

It was getting late, and he didn't want to be a sourpuss in Nasia's company. He stared at her, unsure if he should.

Seeing his hesitation, she continued. "You shouldn't be alone tonight."

He jerked his head in a nod and killed the engine. He got out of the truck and strolled over to her side. He wasn't sure what it was about Nasia, but he was learning pretty fast she was becoming a weakness.

Once in the house, they kicked off their shoes with Nasia leading him by his hand. She tossed her purse on the couch as they bypassed it and guided him into her bedroom.

"Take all of your clothes off and lie on the bed on your stomach." She motioned to the bed.

"What?"

"You heard me." She laughed, backing away from him. "You'll love this."

She sauntered around the room and lit a few candles.

What the hell.

He kept his eyes on her, taking his clothing off.

Low, slow music came on over the speaker that sat on her dresser.

The last item hit the floor, and he stood curiously observing her, turning the lamp off, casting them in the soft candlelight.

"Bed." She pointed toward it.

With a chuckle he did as he was told and laid on his stomach. He gathered a pillow underneath his head and held it in place while he waited. She disappeared into the bathroom. The sounds of cabinets opening met him.

She returned dressed in a short silky robe. Her hair was pulled up into a messy ponytail on top of her head.

"What are you doing?" he asked, taking her in.

"Shhh…" she murmured. In her hand was a soft black sleep mask. She rested it on his head and slid it down over his eyes, blinding him. Nasia's lips brushed his shoulder, dropping a kiss onto his skin.

"Nasia—"

A finger rested on his lips, stopping him.

"I just want to take care of you tonight. Help you relax and take away all of your stresses."

Her finger ran down his spine, eliciting a shiver to course through him. He swallowed hard at the feeling of her fingertip drifting along his back.

"Can I?"

Hell, at the moment, she could do whatever she wanted to do to him.

"Yeah." He cleared his throat.

"Good. Relax. I promise you will enjoy this." The bed shifted under her weight as she moved along the mattress. She helped him get into a better position.

Stan lay there, waiting to see what she was going to do.

A warm thick liquid poured onto his back, followed by her hands. The scent of lavender and roses greeted him.

Her hands explored his back and kneaded the muscles of his shoulders. He slumped down completely into the mattress.

Her small hands were working the tension out of him.

He basked in the feeling of her massaging him.

There had never been anyone who wanted to take the time to care for him. He was used to being the one who thought of everything, provided anything that was needed.

A slight groan slipped from him as her hands went farther down.

Nasia's chuckle was low and shot a jolt of electricity straight to his dick.

The music floating through the air was sensual with the singer speaking of a long-lost love and what they would do to their lover once they found them.

Her fingers dug into the muscles, turning them to mush. She continued to use warm oils that allowed her hands to slip around his skin.

Stan's cock was erect and pushing into the mattress. The need for this woman was growing.

It was quite scary.

He'd never wanted anyone as much as he desired her.

Nasia was always thoughtful and ensured his needs were met.

"You're so tense," she murmured.

His only response he could muster was a grunt.

Her hands skated down to his ass. She worked those muscles, moving down to the backs of his thighs.

He balled the sheets in a tight fist.

Nasia tortured him ever so slowly until she reached his ankles.

The foot massage, mind-blowing.

"Now, turn over," she whispered.

He rolled over, and his cock sprang free, jutting in the air away from his body. He went to remove the eye covering, but small hands stopped him.

"Leave this on. I'm not done."

"What?" he rasped.

Stan's body was strung tight, and he needed her. He tried to reach for Nasia, but she batted his hands away. Her musical laughter floated through the air.

"I'm not done taking care of my man," she breathed.

The bed shifted, and her hands, slick with more oil, trailed along his legs. He swallowed hard when they arrived at his thighs. She kneaded the muscles.

His cock was painfully erect.

Nasia continued up, a throaty moan escaping her. Good.

She was just as affected by this as he was.

He practically skyrocketed from the bed when her hand wrapped around his shaft.

"Nasia," he gasped, reaching down and covering her hand.

He tried to pry her from him, but she wouldn't release him.

"Stop." She chuckled. "Just relax."

Just relax?

He was two seconds from exploding, and she wanted him to relax?

Not fucking likely.

A moan was ripped from him the second her mouth joined the party.

"Fuck," he drew out the word, unable to breathe. He clenched the sheets so tight, he wouldn't be shocked to hear them rip.

She took her time tasting him, guiding his cock in and out of her mouth. Her tongue slid along the length of him, sucking him deep to the back of her throat.

Tremors rippled through him.

The woman was trying to take his soul.

It was hers.

She continued on, bringing him to the brink of his climax. Her hands, mouth, and tongue were very deadly. Wherever her mouth couldn't go, her hand was there. Slipping along the length of him, coated with her saliva.

He writhed underneath her touch, turning his pleasure over to her.

"Nasia," he groaned. He had to warn her that he couldn't hold back any longer. His balls drew close to his body, signaling he was about to explode. He reached his hand out and found the top of her head as it bobbed up and down on his shaft. "I'm about to come."

She tightened her grip on the base of his cock and moved her head even faster.

The only signal she had heard him.

Stan threw his head back and roared, filling her mouth with his seed. Nasia sucked it all down, not stopping for one moment.

The ripples of his orgasm racked his body, draining every ounce of energy from him, unlike anything he'd ever experienced before.

Nasia hadn't stopped. She continued to stroke and suck on his cock which was still hard.

His body grew tense, the air ripped from his lungs.

Oh fuck.

He came again.

Stan fell back against the pillows, his breaths ragged. His body trembled from the aftershocks of his orgasms.

Holy hell.

His blood pounded in his ears. Stan was drained, unable to move.

What the hell had she done to him?

The bed shifted, and Nasia's warm naked body came to lie next to him. She adjusted his arm so she could snuggle in the crook of it. The sleeping mask was removed from his face, but he didn't even know if he had the strength to open his eyes.

Nasia brushed a soft kiss to the corner of his lips.

"Thank you," she whispered.

He turned and pried open his eyes, taking her in. Her dark eyes were watching him, a cocky little smirk on her lips.

"For what?" He cleared his throat, his voice coming out raspy. "Why are you thanking me?"

Her gaze skimmed his chest, and her hand teased the wisps of hair scattered along his skin. A small smile played on her lips. The flickering of the candles highlighted all of her features. She was the most beautiful woman he'd ever seen.

Inside and out.

"For allowing me to take care of you."

"That's not for you to do," he murmured, hugging her closer to him.

"Bullshit." She snorted. Her fingers trailed along

his face, running along his jawline. "I'm not your ex-wife, Stan. I want to provide for your needs, listen to your troubles, help you up when you are low. That's what a couple does in a relationship. It's a two-way street, and the longer I'm with you, the more I want to be a part of every aspect of your life. The good and the bad."

At that moment, he fell in love with her.

He reached for her, drawing her closer and covering her mouth with his in a hard, bruising kiss. They rolled over until she was under him. After two orgasms back to back, he didn't know if his cock would be waking up anytime soon, but that didn't mean he would be denying her the pleasure of his tongue.

❄   9   ❄

"Hey, sis!" Aleka's voice greeted her on her cell.

Nasia instantly grinned. She could feel the excitement radiating from her sister through the phone.

"Please tell me you have good news." Nasia moved around her kitchen, putting her clean dishes up.

She had decided to take a day off. Sara and Tarik were capable to prepping the café and running it. Today, she was going to post for the position of assistant manager in the local paper and online. She'd had a meeting with her accountant yesterday, and according to him, she was in a good position for the addition to the restaurant.

Afterwards, she planned to surprise Stan after he got off work with a good home-cooked meal.

"Did you ever doubt my ability to secure us two tickets, third row from center stage?"

"What?" Nasia shrieked. She hopped up and down in place with excitement. "How did you manage that?"

"Oh, honey. I can't divulge my secrets. You know I know a guy, who knows a guy…" Aleka joked.

Nasia hadn't spoken with her sister about the tickets since they'd initially talked about them. She had figured Aleka hadn't got them. It was all over the news how quick the concert had sold out.

Nasia rolled her eyes. Her heart raced with the thought that she would be so close to Nina Hunt performing.

"I'll book the hotel," Nasia offered. "And how much do I owe you for my ticket?"

"Please. Consider it an early birthday gift."

"Our birthday is in a few months." Nasia closed the pantry and walked over to check on the roast she had in the crockpot to take a peek at it. The scent of it was beginning to fill the kitchen.

"Well, this is all on me," Aleka said. "Why don't I drive down to Shady Springs, then we drive up to Denver together for the concert."

"But I had thought I would just drive up. That way you don't have to waste gas coming down this way." Nasia leaned against the counter and took in her kitchen. It was finally clean, and she needed to jump in the shower.

Shady Springs was located forty miles south of Colorado Springs. The drive to Denver was a little over two hours.

"It will be fun. I'll drive down on Thursday night, then we can drive up here Friday, concert on Saturday, then I'll take you back home on Sunday. It will be a fun girls' weekend."

A weekend with her sister would be fun. It had been a while since they had spent time together.

"All righty then." Nasia giggled. Knowing her little sister, they would be heavy in their cups and screaming all of Nina's songs at the top of their lungs on performance night. They were both die-hard fans of the singer.

"Wear your sluttiest outfit. Oh, wait. You have a man now." Aleka groaned.

"I sure do. He's the only one who is privy to see my slutty outfits," Nasia teased. She pushed off the counter and headed toward her bedroom.

"And when do I get to meet this cowboy, who I've

barely heard anything about?" There was a hint of hurt in her sister's voice.

"Well, you will hear all about him on girls' weekend."

"I better. I want to hear everything. From how big his dick is, does he know how to use it, and if he has a brother."

Nasia barked a laugh. She stripped her clothes off, dropping them into the hamper in her closet.

"His dick is none of your business, and yes, he has a brother. A younger one." She moved into the bathroom and turned on the shower to allow it to warm up.

"We used to be real close and share everything." There was a pout in Aleka's voice.

Her sister was right. They had told each other everything when they were younger, but now something was different.

Sharing personal things about what went on between her and Stan seemed like an invasion of their privacy. Their intimate details should remain just between the two of them.

"He means something to me," she admitted, putting her phone on speaker. She put her shower cap on.

"Aww...is my big sister in love?"

Nasia paused and thought about the question.

Was she?

She thought back to the night they had gone bowling with the other couples. On the way home, listening to him had brought about a strong urge to help erase the darkness clouding him. That bitch of an ex-wife was playing mind games, and Nasia wanted to draw him back to her.

That night would be forever cherished in her memory.

Something had passed between them.

He had made love to her with a fury that night. By morning, neither of them had the strength to move. They hadn't dragged themselves out of bed until mid-morning.

"I think I am," she murmured.

"Well, then I shall have to meet this fella of yours. I can't wait."

"I can't wait for you to meet him, too. You'll like him."

"Well, I hear your shower running. Go ahead and go. I'm sure you stink."

"Bitch."

"You love this bitch," Aleka taunted.

"I do. Bye." Nasia hit the red button on her

phone's screen to end the call. A silly grin was on her face.

Love Stan?

Who was she kidding?

She was head over heels in love with that man.

WEARY, STAN HEADED TOWARD HIS TRUCK. Today had been a big day at the ranch. It was going on eight at night, and with him arriving at work at five-thirty that morning, it meant for a long day. His gaze landed on the gleaming black paint and detail of his newly acquired truck.

He had finally bitten the bullet and purchased a brand-new Dodge Ram. It was a thing of beauty. Five minutes sitting in the truck, and he felt a connection. It had a quad cab to allow him to have plenty of room inside along with all the bells and whistles that Laney didn't have.

This was his first brand-new vehicle purchase, and he was exited. Now he had to figure out what his new truck's name was.

His back pocket vibrated just as he arrived at the driver's door. He snatched his phone out and looked at the screen to see who was calling.

Victoria.

"What the hell?" He rolled his eyes and contemplated not answering it. He hadn't the last two times she'd called. He might as well get this over with and see what she wanted.

He ran his finger across the glass screen.

"What?" He opened the door and slid into the driver's seat. The plush leather was so comforting.

"Well, hello to you, too," Victoria's soft voice came on the line.

"Victoria, what do you want?" He hit the button to start the engine. It roared to life, and his heart skipped a beat. The lavish interior was more than he'd ever had, and he was still getting used to the technology that came with it. The call flipped over to the hands-free mode in the truck.

Stan removed his Stetson and set it in the passenger seat. He pushed a hand through his sweat-soaked hair. He grimaced, scenting himself.

It wasn't good either.

He wasn't sure what would smell worse, him or a heaping pile of cow dung.

"I was wondering if you wanted to go out for lunch or something." She paused.

He grew still, unable to believe what he had just heard.

"Victoria, no."

"I was serious, Stan. We can work this out."

"I'm hanging up, Victoria." He shifted his truck into gear and drove along the dirt road that led onto the main street. He passed Jonah's house on the Blazing Eagle Ranch. He was sure Jonah, the Brooks brothers' father, was inside at this hour. He had finally recovered from his heart attack that had almost killed him. The stubborn older man wasn't going to let a little thing like blocked coronary arteries take him out.

"Why won't you at least talk with me?"

"Because I don't have to. You gave up that right," he stated matter-of-factly. The only reason he would want to hear from her was if one of her parents had become severely ill or passed away. He'd had a pretty good relationship with them over the years. They were even embarrassed Stan and Victoria had divorced because of their child's infidelity.

"You're still dating that woman?"

"None of your business," he snapped.

"But, Stan, I'm your wife. We were together—"

"Key words should be 'was my wife.' Again, you gave up all rights to any part of my life. Goodbye, Vicki." He disconnected the call.

She hated the shortened version of her name. She

made sure to correct everyone that her name was Victoria not Vicki.

Blowing out a deep breath, he leaned back and concentrated on the road. His phone rang again. He hit the button as soon as he saw it was Nasia.

"Hey, babe," he answered.

"Hey, there," her melodic voice came over the speakers, immediately relaxing him. "You just now leaving work?"

"Yeah." He sighed.

"You sound tired."

"Tired don't even begin to describe it. Not even sure how I'm driving."

"Why didn't you stay at the ranch?"

"Because I want my bed, or yours." He smirked.

"Well, if you come here, I'm sure you won't be sleeping." Her voice dropped low and dripped sex.

He hardened and knew she was correct. The second he walked through the door of her home, he wouldn't even think of sleep. The sex between them was explosive and addicting. He couldn't keep his hand off her body.

"Just head home," she said. "We can see each other tomorrow."

He grimaced. Tomorrow wouldn't even be better. There were plenty of things that needed doing on the ranch. From repairing equipment to starting pregnancy testing female cows and vaccinating them. Dr. Hutson was scheduled to stop by. This was the time where they prepared for the winter.

"I may have to take a raincheck on tomorrow," he admitted.

"That's fine, baby. I know you're busy. I understand. My sister is supposed be coming down. She surprised me and got tickets to the Nina Hunt concert up in Denver." Her voice ended on a shriek.

"Really? That's awesome." He chuckled at her excitement. "I didn't know you had planned to go to the concert."

"I didn't either. She called me out of the blue. We had talked about it a while ago, and frankly, I had forgotten all about it until she called me and told me she was able to get tickets."

"So are you driving up to meet her?" He scratched his head. They had spoken about their families, and he would love to go meet them. Nasia had a few pictures around her home with her family, but it wasn't the same as meeting them and getting to know them in person.

"I had planned to, but she's talking crazy about coming here to pick me up so we can go together, but that makes no sense whatsoever." Nasia giggled.

"I'm going to talk her out of it and just drive up there."

"Well, I'm happy for you." He turned down his street and took notice of a car in his driveway. The hairs on the back of his neck rose.

It couldn't be.

"Have you thought of a new name for the truck yet?" Nasia's voice broke through his thoughts.

He stared hard and slowed his vehicle down.

What the fuck?

Victoria was sitting on his steps.

"Nasia, let me call you back. I'm pulling in now." He hated to cut their call short. He loved speaking with her on the ride home if they weren't seeing each other that day. Now seeing Victoria at his house, he should have just gone to Nasia's.

"Okay. You got home pretty fast. Call me later."

"I will."

The call disconnected. 'I love you' was on the tip of his tongue. He bit it back, not wanting the first time he told her to be on the telephone. It had to be a special moment for such powerful words.

He parked his truck next to Victoria's sedan.

"I ain't got time for this bullshit," he muttered. He snagged his Stetson resting on the passenger seat and exited the truck. He opened the back door and grabbed his duffle bag off the seat and hefted it onto his shoulder. "What are you doing here?"

Victoria stood from her perch, brushing off the back of her jeans.

"We need to talk, and you hung up on me. All I'm asking is for us to just speak with each other, hash out problems."

"Victoria, we've been divorced almost a year, and now you want to talk and hash out problems? That should have been done before you decided to spread your legs for Connor."

"Stan," she sputtered, her face growing flushed.

He walked around her, but her small hand latched on to his arm.

"Please, Stan," she pleaded, tears in her voice.

Stan's heart was hardened from what she'd put him through. He turned around and glared at her. He didn't care they were in the front yard where his nosy neighbors could see or hear them. If she wanted to hash shit out now, they were doing it now.

"I fucked up. I know that," she said. "I'm so sorry for everything I've done. For the hurt I've caused you, but I really want us to sit down and try again." Tears streamed down her cheeks. She pushed her blonde hair behind her ears. Her chin trembled where she clearly was trying not to sob.

Stan didn't feel a thing. Her tears used to cause him to be frantic. He was the fix-it type of guy. If something was wrong, he would right it. He had worked so hard for them that her betrayal cut him deep.

"What do you want me to say? Are you here seeking forgiveness?"

"I want you back!" she screamed. She slapped a hand over her mouth, her eyes widened. She blinked and removed her hand. "Stan, please. Let me come in so we can talk."

He stalked to her, stopping inches from her. All of the anger and hurt that was buried inside him was threatening to boil over. He was never a man to raise his hand to a woman, but he wasn't above giving her a piece of his mind.

"You don't get to come back in my life and demand that we get back together. You fucked up. You ended our marriage. There was plenty of things that you—we—could have done when we were married. You didn't open up to me then, you took the first compliment another man gave you and spread your fucking legs—"

Her hand connected with his face, his cheek stinging slightly.

She gasped and took a step back.

He stared off down the street, thanking the man upstairs that his parents raised him to be a real man. He flicked his gaze back to her and shook his head.

"Truth hurts, don't it." He growled, tightening his grip on the handle of his bag. He straightened to his full height. "I think you should go now."

He spun around on his heel, pulling his keys from his pocket.

"Wait!" Victoria cried out. "I'm so sorry. I don't know what came over me."

She was outright sobbing at the moment. At one point, he would have responded, invited her in and listened to what she had to say.

Not today.

Stan reached the door, ignoring her. He opened it and went in, shutting it behind him.

10

"**B**ig sister!" Aleka shouted, rushing through the front door. Even though Nasia was a few minutes older, Aleka always called her 'big sister.' Which she was, and there was never a day Nasia didn't remind her twin of this.

Aleka kicked off her shoes and flew to Nasia, wrapping her arms around her. She was acting like it had been years since they had last seen each other.

Nasia did have to admit it felt good for her sister to be there.

"How was the drive?" Nasia returned Aleka's hug.

"Not bad at all. I mean, my foot stayed on the gas so I got here in record time."

Nasia chuckled, shutting the door, and followed her sister into her house.

"I can still crash in your office, right?" Aleka set her suitcase by the couch.

"Yup. I still don't know why you are driving down here wasting your gas." Nasia flopped down on her couch and tucked her feet underneath her.

"Well, there was an alternative motive for me being here." Aleka grinned.

"I figured." Nasia rolled her eyes.

They were identical twins, and there were very slight differences between them that only their parents could tell them apart if they dressed alike. They had different style of clothing, men, careers, but one thing that remained similar between them was their hair.

Both of them preferred to wear it flat ironed bone-straight. Lately, Nasia was allowing Yani to be a little bold and put her hair in new styles.

"A few friends from high school are getting together tonight for drinks. Remember Shante?"

"Umm…yeah. Wasn't she the one that was on the volleyball team and got hit in the face and broke her nose?" Even though they were twins, they hung out with different crowds. It was hard to forget a girl walking around school with a busted nose and two black eyes for a while.

"Yes, she's in town this week from Miami. She moved there about five years ago, and the girls want to take her out since she's back." Aleka grinned.

"That sounds fun." A yawn escaped Nasia. She was feeling the effects of working long hours. She couldn't wait until she was at the point where she didn't have to stay from open to close at the café. Thankfully the café closed at five each day. Once she hired on an assistant manager, then she could pull back a little.

"Why don't you come with us."

Nasia shook her head. These were Aleka's friends. She remembered a few of the other ones that Aleka mentioned would be going, but she just didn't have it in her.

"Are you sure?" Aleka pouted.

"No, I'm sorry. I'm staying in tonight. With us leaving for the weekend, I'm going to get up earlier and head into the café so I can get some prep work done so my team won't have too much to do."

Already that three-thirty alarm was looming in the back of her head.

"Yeah, yeah. I get it. I may not like it, but my sister, the boss, must be responsible." Aleka hopped up and grabbed the handle of her suitcase and dragged it behind her as she disappeared down the hallway.

Nasia stretched out on the couch and snagged her blanket from the edge. She picked up the remote and flipped the television on. She surfed the channels until she came to a movie that she loved. She had her favorites that she watched every time they came on.

"Chicken good," she echoed, saying the lines along with the orange-haired woman on the screen. Nasia giggled, recognizing she probably knew the movie by heart.

Soon her sister was emerging from the back dressed up for a night on the town.

"Look at you." Nasia grinned. Her sister looked like a million bucks. "Where you get that shirt from?"

"From this new boutique that's around the corner from my apartment." Aleka twirled around to show off her outfit.

"Why you ain't get me one?" Nasia teased.

They fell into a fit of laughter. It had been years since they'd dressed alike, but the shirt and jeans were cute. They still wore the same size, and Nasia will have to borrow that shirt.

"Last chance." Aleka focused her wide puppy-dog eyes on Nasia who shook her head.

"I can't. I've got to do boss things in the morning." Nasia pushed off the couch and followed her sister to the door.

"Don't wait up," Aleka joked, skipping out the door.

"You still have your key?" Nasia called out. She leaned on the door, watching her sister walk to her car.

"I do." Aleka dug around in her purse, brandishing the extra set of keys that Nasia had given her.

Nasia stayed at the door until Aleka drove off down the road. She shut the door and went back into the living room. A sigh escaped her. She snagged her cell phone off the couch and shot a text to Stan that she was turning in to bed early and she'd see him in the morning for breakfast.

His response was almost immediate.

Sleep well, baby.

Nasia smiled. She turned off the television and left the lamp in the corner on so the house won't be dark when Aleka returned home.

Going back to her bedroom, she responded.

I will dream of you.

She placed her phone on the nightstand and stripped off her clothes. Morning was going to come soon enough. She turned on her television to the movie she'd been watching.

Within minutes, jammies were on, her hair was wrapped, and she was climbing in the bed. Checking her phone, she saw another message from Stan.

See you in the morning.

Nasia smiled and set her phone back on the charge. A yawn overtook her. She snuggled down under the covers, the movie still playing. Her eyes began to feel gritty, her body relaxed, so she gave in and allowed sleep to take a hold of her.

SOFT COUNTRY MUSIC PLAYED. STAN yawned, guiding his truck out of his driveway. The mornings were coming quicker every day.

The ranch had been extremely busy. By the time he got home it was late, he was sore all over, and he wouldn't have been good company if he had gone over to Nasia's house.

So, he went home, ate, showered, and crashed.

Now he was back up, having to do it all over again. Today, he got up earlier to he could get to the

Blazing Eagle early to help with repairs on one of the barns. It was an overhaul job and would take pretty much all day.

Stan was never one to back away from hard labor. He couldn't remember the last time he took some time off from work.

It had to be about three years ago when he and Victoria had gone to Jamaica. She had fussed and said she wanted them to go somewhere far away from ranches and small towns. She demanded to go somewhere warm and near an ocean. He had her book the trip to make her happy, and they left Colorado for a full ten days.

It had been nice and relaxing.

What he wouldn't give right now to be somewhere with Nasia. Just the two of them alone, a beach, and Nasia dressed in a little two-piece for his eyes only.

A beach, his woman, and a cold beer.

That would be the perfect vacation.

He wondered if he could talk Nasia into going away for a bit. She worked so hard and was stubborn as a mule.

Glancing down at the time on the truck's display monitor, he saw that it was her usual leaving time.

He turned the truck in the direction of her house and pressed down harder on the gas.

He'd go over and meet her at her house and follow her to the café. He really enjoyed their short time together in the morning before work. It was something that helped him get through the grueling work hours.

Arriving at her street, he slowed down to not put his truck on two wheels while turning on the corner.

A grin teased his lips at the thought of seeing her. This weekend she was going up to Denver with her sister for a concert, and he was going to miss her something fierce. It was amazing in such a quick time they had fallen in sync with each other.

The light on Nasia's garage was on.

That's strange.

A car was parked at the edge of the driveway. A tall man was leaning against the vehicle with a small woman trapped against it.

Stan coasted to a halt, pulling the car over to the awning. He cut the light and couldn't help but stare at the couple.

His pulse pounded in his ears.

It couldn't be.

Not Nasia.

Stan ran a trembling hand along his face,

watching the couple in a deep, passionate embrace. He couldn't tear his gaze away from them.

If it was any other person being molested by a man, Stan would turn away, embarrassed.

But no.

Bile threatened to erupt from him. He swallowed hard, unable to believe his eyes, but then again, he was looking dead at her.

You're always working. When do you have time for me?

Victoria's voice echoed in his mind. Stan rested back on the headrest and closed his eyes. His chest tightened, a deep pain spreading through his body.

He didn't want to believe Nasia would cheat on him.

Opening his eyes, he watched her lead the guy up to her house. She inserted the key and tugged him inside.

The door shut, leaving Stan to stare at it in disbelief.

But why wouldn't Nasia go seek out someone else?

It was almost the same situation as when he'd caught Victoria in bed with Connor. Only this time, he wouldn't see another man worshipping the body of the woman he had come to love.

Someone else had taken his place.

Again.

He should have learned the first time, but apparently, he was just too hard-headed.

Blowing out a deep breath, he sat up straight and put the truck back in drive. He flipped the lights and hit the gas. The screeching of the wheels pierced the air. He ignored it, driving away, leaving his heart behind.

"Not anymore," he muttered. His hands hurt from how hard he gripped the steering wheel.

He'd throw himself into the one thing that had never let him down.

Work.

This was it for him.

No more attempts at relationships.

The hope, love, and desire to have a future with a beautiful brown-skinned woman died inside him.

Turning onto the highway, he focused on the road ahead of him. He'd have to push down all the emotions in him and lock them away for good.

11

Nasia yawned for what seemed like the millionth time. Aleka was as stubborn as they come. Nasia couldn't talk her sister into just letting her drive up and meet her at her house. They could have then driven over to Denver from Aurora.

But no.

Of course she had another reason for coming to Shady Springs. She just should have said so from the get-go.

When Nasia had woken up to get ready to come to the café there was no sign of her twin. As the elder sister, Nasia had been worried about Aleka. Before she'd climbed in her car, she had sent off a text to Aleka to make sure she was alive.

She knew her sister would be fine, but it was late —early—and there was still no sign of her.

Aleka immediately responded that she would be coming home soon.

Nasia had an office that doubled as a spare room, which was used by her sister whenever she came to visit.

Satisfied her sister was okay, she'd left for work.

Coming in earlier than normal had been a great idea. She had gotten so much prep done.

Anxiety filled her at the thought of being away from the Shady Bean for a few days. Tarik and Sara swore they would be fine. They would rotate who opened and closed, along with the part-timers. She had a great staff who she had grown close with.

Nasia had submitted for the assistant manager position online and in the paper, and she had a few responses with a couple interviews lined up next week.

Nasia poured the perfect amount of dry ingredients into the large mixer. She flipped it on to mix them gently, but her fingers slipped and switched it to high.

Flour flew everywhere.

Nasia screeched, flipping the switch to off.

Glancing down at herself, she giggled. Flour was

all over her shirt, apron, and pants. She was sure it was on her face as well.

Too tired to even brush it off, she turned around, needing more caffeine. She apparently wasn't awake enough. She'd been at work for hours now and had only one cup of coffee.

That would not do.

She passed a mirror on the wall in the hall and paused.

"Shit," she breathed. She looked like Casper the Ghost. She brushed as much of the flour from her hair as she could. Using the edge of her apron, she wiped her face clean. "A little better."

Continuing on, she went out into the main part of the café and went behind the counter.

Stan hadn't stopped by for their early morning chat.

That was strange, but Nasia wasn't worried. He said they were extremely busy at the ranch, and she figured he went straight in to get work done.

"Ugh," Nasia groaned. There were quite a few people in line. The café was buzzing. Upbeat music played, streaming from the speakers around the shop.

"Who won the fight, you or the flour?" Tarik

joked. He handed the woman at the counter her change and turned to Nasia.

"Flour can't take me," she grinned. She snagged a cup and poured herself a hefty amount of coffee. Inhaling the delicious aroma, she doctored it to her liking.

"Need any help out here?" Nasia placed a plastic top on her cup.

"Nope, we're good." Lark smiled, making the drink orders.

She was a part-timer who Nasia hoped she could hire on full time. After she got the assistant manager position filled, she should be able to offer Lark more hours. The Shady Bean was doing extremely well and growing.

"I could restock for you—"

"I just did it," Tarik said.

"Well, you two have everything worked out." Nasia laughed. She took a sip of her coffee and walked from behind the counter. When she had the chance, she liked to greet the patrons. She wanted everyone to feel comfortable coming into her café, and this allowed her to get to know the townsfolk.

"Morning," Nasia greeted an older man sitting at a table drinking his coffee and reading the paper.

He looked up at her and gave her a toothy grin. "Nasia, how the hell are you?"

Now that she was looking him in the eyes, she remembered him. Mr. Waite, her high school history teacher.

"Mr. Waite, I'm well. How are you?" She smiled widely at him.

"Swell, darling. This is a mighty fine place you got here." He tipped his cup to her.

"Thanks. It's always been a dream of mine," she admitted.

"I knew you would do well in life, young lady. You always had ambition." He took a sip of his drink and let out a sigh. "And you have the best coffee in town."

"Thanks. Are you still teaching?" she asked.

"I retired just last year. Me and the missus have bought an RV, and we go out for months at a time traveling the country." He sat back, proud of his accomplishment.

Nasia couldn't wait for the day she could retire and spend her days doing whatever she chose.

Her and Stan—

She froze.

Yeah, she could see herself with Stan together in the future. She was in love with him and she would continue to work on him until they had solidified their future together.

There was no other man for her.

"Well, that sounds amazing. Be sure to bring her by. We have pastries I'm sure she would love."

"Oh, I've purchased and took them home to her. She loves your baking." He chuckled.

She glanced around, and her gaze landed on a certain figure sitting at a table near the door.

Victoria.

"Have a nice day, Mr. Waite. I need to make my rounds."

"Go ahead, young lady. I don't mean to tie you up." He gave her a nod and turned back to his paper.

Nasia stood up straighter and headed over to Victoria. She didn't know what the woman was doing here, but Nasia was about to find out.

The blonde had a coffee and pastry sitting on the table, and she wrote in what appeared to be a journal.

"Morning." Nasia stood next to the table.

Victoria looked up at her with the phoniest smile Nasia had ever seen. The woman was up to something.

"Nasia, you have a unique little shop." Victoria put her pen down and picked up her coffee.

"I'm going to take that as a compliment." Nasia held her coffee cup with both hands to ward off any temptations to scratch Victoria's eyes out.

This woman had done a number on Stan.

That poor handsome man was filled with so many doubts because of her.

"Oh, it was." Victoria grinned. "Stan told me the coffee here was the best he's ever had."

"Oh?" That was news to Nasia. When would Stan recommend her coffee to his ex-wife?

"Yes. We've spoken several times, and he suggested I try you out."

Nasia narrowed her eyes on the woman.

The woman may not want to 'try' Nasia out.

"I hope you don't mind if I sit down." Nasia motioned to the chair across from Victoria.

"By all means, you own the restaurant." Victoria shrugged.

"You've spoken several times with my man? About what?"

"Oh, you mean my husband—"

"Ex-husband," Nasia corrected.

Victoria rolled her eyes and waved her hand. "Listen, Stan and I were together a long time. Mistakes were made, and when adults come together to sit down, leaving all emotions at the door, things can get worked out."

"Is that so?" Nasia took a sip of her coffee to busy herself.

"Yes. Stan is a forgiving man, and now that time has passed, we were able to talk about the issues in our marriage."

"You mean how you jumped on his friend's dick?"

Victoria froze in place, staring at Nasia. She visibly swallowed hard and glanced down at her cup, then met Nasia's eyes. "Yes, Stan and I discussed everything, and we are talking about getting back together."

"Cut the bullshit," Nasia snapped. She lowered her voice, not wanting to draw attention to them. "I know Stan, and he would never get back with you."

There was nothing this woman could say that would make Nasia believe her. She would have to hear it from Stan before she accepted what she'd heard.

"Look, Nasia." Victoria leaned forward, resting her forearms on the table.

Nasia wanted to slap the fake smile off her lips.

"You may think you know Stan, but you don't.

You're just a passing fancy for him. A rebound as he waited for me to come back to him."

Did this bitch just call me the rebound?

Nasia set her cup down on the table.

"Is that so?" Nasia murmured. She prayed for restraint, and to keep her from reaching across the table and putting her hands on the woman.

"Yes, so I'm going to ask you kindly to stay away from my husband."

"You're funny." Nasia snorted. She eased back and met Victoria's gaze. "Stan's my man, and you're a little bit deranged if you think he's coming back to you. And as for me knowing Stan, I know him very well, in every sense a man and woman can know each other."

Victoria's face grew flushed. Her smile disappeared as she fidgeted in her seat.

"And I can tell you when he's with me, you're the last thing on his mind while he's fucking me. Which is quite often." Nasia stood from her seat and gave Victoria a curt smile. "Can I get you a refill?"

STAN IGNORED THE VIBRATION IN HIS BACK pocket. He was sure it was Nasia. He didn't want to speak with her at the moment. Eventually he would have to, but now, he couldn't. He couldn't get the sight of her leading another man into her home from his mind.

For some reason, her betrayal cut deeper than finding Victoria's body entwined with Conner's.

He had thought they had something special between them. She had ensured she'd 'claimed him' as she had said. Everything between them had to be genuine.

At least he had thought it was.

Maybe it was being hurt from Victoria that he'd latched on to the first woman who'd showed him attention in ways he was not used to.

Nasia was new. Fresh. With curves in all the right places. Stan would have to admit, he always did appreciate a curvy womanly frame. Victoria was slender and may weigh a buck twenty when wet.

Stan entered the barn and headed to the bunkers. He was too tired to go home and he didn't want to chance running into Victoria or Nasia.

So instead of going home, he was going to hide out on the ranch.

"Not going home?" Rashad called out as he walked out of the stall where his horse, Brandy, resided.

"Nope. We got too much work to do in the morning." He hefted his duffle bag strap higher on his shoulder.

"Ain't that the truth. But I prefer the arms of my woman than those hard-ass bunks." Rashad chuckled.

Stan forced a smile and gave his friend a salute. He continued on and disappeared down the hall where the sleeping rooms were. There were five rooms with twin bunks in each. Stan entered the last room and shut the door behind him.

He leaned back against the door, trying to push down the feeling of anxiety in his chest. Taking his Stetson off, he pushed off the door. He dropped his hat down on the table next to the bed and tossed his bag on the top bunk.

His phone rang again. He picked it up and glanced at the display.

Nasia.

He tossed it onto the bed and allowed the call to go to voicemail.

Stan stripped down to his boxer briefs and headed to the shower room.

He just wanted to be left alone.

$$\begin{array}{ccc} \text{\reflectbox{?}} & 12 & \text{?} \end{array}$$

"Stan, baby, It's me. Where are you?" Nasia sighed. She closed her eyes and tucked a wayward strand of her hair behind her ear. "Call me when you get this."

She set her phone down on her desk and rested her head in her hands. Her office was quiet, but the sounds of the café were muffled by her door. Dread filled her, and she couldn't shake the feeling.

Stan hadn't accepted any of her phone calls since last week. The last time she'd had any communication with him was their text messages where she had told him to stay home.

After her confrontation with Victoria, she had tried calling him. He hadn't answered, but she attributed it to him being busy at work and he couldn't answer.

So she finished her day up at the café and went home. She and Aleka had driven up to Denver for one hell of a concert. Nina Hunt was one amazing performer and was worth every penny.

As much fun as she had with her sister, she couldn't shake that something was wrong.

She returned to Shady Springs and no word from him.

Was Victoria telling her the truth? Were they getting back together, and this was his way of distancing himself from her?

Nasia refused to believe that. Stan was a man who believed in honesty. He would have told her himself if he was getting back with his ex-wife.

Nasia lifted her head at the knock sounding at the door.

"Come in," she called out. She straightened up and wiggled the computer mouse to wake up her computer screen which had gone dark.

"Everything okay, boss?" Sara popped her head in. Her eyes were wide and filled with curiosity.

"Yeah, just tired," Nasia lied. She offered up a smile, but it was obvious Sara didn't believe her.

"The woman you were supposed to interview,

Ellie, just called and said she needed to cancel. Her babysitter didn't show. She wanted to know if she could come same time tomorrow."

Well, that wasn't a good sign for an interviewee. Nasia opened up her calendar on her computer to pull up tomorrow's schedule.

She would be free.

"That's fine," Nasia replied.

"Okay, I'll let her know." Sara paused in the doorway, tilting her head to the side. "You're sure you're good? It looks as if there was something bothering you."

"I just wished I would have taken some more time off," Nasia said. That was partially true. She had been working nonstop since she'd moved to Shady Springs.

"You should have. We would have made it work here. You've trained us all well, we can follow recipes, and we all know you need time away from this place." Sara leaned against the doorjamb.

"I appreciate you all," Nasia said. "I promise I will take a real vacation soon."

"We're going to hold you to it." Sara tossed her a wink, disappearing through the door. It closed behind her with a soft click.

Nasia grabbed her phone and dialed her sister.

She needed to speak with someone she could trust, and there was no one else on the planet that she knew wouldn't judge her other than Aleka.

"Hey, sis. What's up?" Aleka's cheery voice came onto the line.

"I think I fucked up, but I don't know how," she admitted.

"What on earth are you talking 'bout?"

"Stan isn't taking my calls." Nasia pouted, fear taking over her. Was it over between them? Why wouldn't he at least speak with her to tell her?

"What do you mean?"

"When I call, he doesn't answer." Unshed tears blurred her vision. She blinked and felt the warm trail of tears on her cheeks. She hadn't cried over a man since she was a young teen, sobbing because her crush hadn't asked her out to the homecoming dance.

"When did this start?" Her sister's voice grew serious.

"In Denver. I haven't spoken with him since the night before we left for the concert."

"That's weird, and he's not even telling you any reason why he's giving you the cold shoulder?"

"No. That's the worst part. I'm left in the dark, guessing."

"Well, maybe it wasn't time for you to settle down," Aleka said. "Maybe what you need is just a fuck buddy. No strings attached. Just someone to rearrange your guts—"

"Aleka!" Nasia wiped her cheeks and shook her head. What was she to do with her twin?

"I'm just saying, like me and Killian."

"Killian? From high school?"

"Yes. Girl, I didn't get to tell you that we hooked up that night I went out for girls' night."

"How did you forget to tell me that?" Nasia asked. Now it was her turn to be a little hurt by her sister keeping something from her.

"Long story short, we came back to your place—"

"My place?" Nasia gasped.

"Yes, you weren't home, and we stayed in my room. I even washed the sheets and comforter," her sister teased.

"I thank you, but seriously, Killian?" He had been the captain of the football team their senior year and had been a real asshole.

"He's just as fine, if not hotter, and let me tell you, it was best you weren't home. My throat was sore from all the screaming before we got to the concert. That's why I barely have a voice now."

"Okay. Can we get back to my problem, please?"

Nasia rolled her eyes. She was happy for her sister that she got to have a dick appointment while in town, but she had much bigger problems on her hands.

"That's what I was trying to say. You need a new man. What kind of man is Stan to not break up with you face to face? Just nothing? No word. That's not a man," Aleka snapped.

They were extremely defensive of each other. They always looked out for one another. It was second nature. Even though Aleka was younger by mere minutes, sometimes she acted as if she were the elder of the two.

"Hey, watch it now. He's my man."

"Are we sure?"

Her sister never held back.

And her question had Nasia stumped.

Was he?

STAN ENTERED THE FARMHOUSE DINER. IT was one of his regular places to eat. The owners boasted that everything in their kitchen came from local farmers. The theme was farm and ranch life and had everything in the restaurant to give it a barn feeling.

Today he didn't have to be at the ranch and had a few errands to run. Grabbing a bite was one of them. He hadn't been eating well after watching Nasia with that man. The scene played on repeat in his mind, and he had to find a way to get it out.

One trick that worked was exhaustion. He'd been working so much at the ranch that he crashed afterwards then got up early in the morning and did it all over again.

"Hey, Stan. Your usual table?" Mindy asked. She was a long-time server at the diner, and they were on a first-name basis. The Farmhouse Diner was one of the first diner's he'd tried out when he had moved to Shady Springs.

After his divorce, his visitations increased.

"Yup." He followed her to his favorite table in the back of the restaurant. It sat along the row of windows that gave him a perfect view of the down-town street. It was a block away from Nasia's café. As much as he wanted to see her, confront her, and demand an explanation, he just couldn't.

From his experience, lies would be all he heard.

He took his seat. Mindy got his drink order and

placed a menu down in front of him with the promise to return.

He glanced over it, contemplating whether he should deviate from his normal order. They had great food, but Stan was a simple man.

"Here's your Coke." Mindy set it down and placed a straw next to the glass. "Ordering your usual, or are you going to be adventurous today?"

"Well, what's the special for the day?" He fiddled with the laminated menu, his gaze roaming it one last time.

"Country fried steak with two sides."

It sounded good, but that wasn't something he'd want for lunch.

"Give me my usual." He laughed, handing her the menu.

"Double cheeseburger with all the works, loaded fries with extra chili on them," she recited from memory and wrote it down. "All right, suga. It shouldn't be too long."

Mindy walked away, leaving Stan alone. He took off his Stetson and put it on the booth next to him. He stared down at his phone and wondered if he should just call Nasia or stop by her house. Maybe he should admit that he saw her with the other man and see what she had to say.

He was going to need closure.

Another relationship down the drain, and this one hadn't taken years to implode.

"Is this seat taken?"

Stan glanced up, finding Victoria standing by the table. He swore he was seeing her more now than when they were married.

"How the hell did you know where I am?" He narrowed his gaze on her as she slid into the booth in front of him.

She held up her phone and smiled. "You are still sharing your location to my phone from yours."

"So you've been stalking me?" He filed a note in the back of his mind to block her on his phone.

"No, I was doing some shopping and thought of you. I figured you might be at work, but to my surprise you were here. I remember how much you liked coming here." She smiled softly. "You, Stan Larsen, are a creature of habit."

"Well, you can go ahead and forget my habits," he grumbled. He shoved a hand through his hair and glanced out the window. Pedestrians made their way along the sidewalk. It was a nice day for fall. The air was crisp, but the sun was still shining brightly. "What do you want?"

"I just want to have lunch with you," she replied

softly. Victoria leaned forward, resting her elbows on the table. "Nothing else. Just share a meal with you and catch up."

He studied her. She had her hair in a low ponytail and was dressed in a burnt-orange sweater and jeans.

But she wasn't the woman he wanted to be sharing a meal together with.

"Oh, I didn't know you were expecting someone," Mindy said, stopping by the table. She turned to Victoria. "Hey, Vicki. What can I get you?"

"It's Victoria," she said, a frown marring her features.

Stan knew Mindy called her by the nickname on purpose. He was sure the entire town had known about their divorce. It was a small enough community where news spread like wildfire.

"Of course. How silly of me to forget." Mindy rolled her eyes and giggled. "Can I get you something?"

"Diet Coke and a chopped salad with Italian dressing," Victoria replied.

Stan cleared his throat and stared at her. She had never been one to be adventurous when it came to food either. When they went out to restaurants, it was always a salad. She always worried about her figure and worked out constantly.

"So what do you want to talk about?" he asked.

"Dad retired finally," she announced.

"Good for him."

"Mom says that since he's been home with her, she's close to putting him out." She laughed.

Stan smiled. Her parents, Barb and Jim, were good people. He had never had the issues with crazy in-laws. He hadn't minded spending time with them when they'd stopped by their home. They still lived in Shady Springs. He may give Jim a call to wish him well on retirement.

"I'm sure he's just tinkering away in his garage and she's not used to him being there during the day so much."

Jim owned one of the automotive service shops on the outskirts of town. He opened a few other locations in towns located not too far from Shady Springs. If he'd retired, Stan assumed Victoria's brother had inherited leadership of the business.

"Yeah. He's taken it upon himself to start doing all the repairs around the house and getting in her way." Victoria chuckled.

"Here you go," Mindy interrupted. She set her tray on the table next to them and began placing their plates in front of them.

The aroma of the chili fries and burger hit Stan,

and his stomach growled, reminding him how hungry was.

"Anything else I can get you?" Mindy asked.

Stan glanced around the table and found he had everything he needed. "We're good, thanks."

"Holler if you need anything." Mindy grabbed her tray and took off.

"A creature of habit." Victoria pointed to his food.

"What can I say? It's good." He shrugged, a small smile playing on his lips. He didn't care what anyone thought, he enjoyed the food he liked. If it's not broke, don't fix it.

Someone stopped by their table, and he glanced over and froze.

Nasia.

She was as beautiful as ever. Her hair was in two braids on each side of her head. She was dressed in a warm gray sweater that stopped mid-thigh, leggings, and riding boots.

The small dark smudges underneath her eyes caught his attention, and for a second he felt horrible, somehow knowing he had put them there.

He swallowed hard, but the memory of her leading that man into her home came rushing back.

"Hello." She smiled, but it didn't reach her eyes.

"Well, hello, Nasia." Victoria placed her fork

down on the table and reached for her napkin, blotting her lips.

"Nasia." He was tongue-tied, not knowing what to say.

"I don't want to keep you from your meal." Nasia ignored Victoria. "But I guess what Victoria told me is true and why you're avoiding me. I just want to say message received." She spun around and dashed through the restaurant toward the door.

"What the hell you say to her?" he growled.

"Nothing that won't be true soon." She shrugged, trying to appear innocent. She picked her fork up and stabbed at a tomato.

Stan flew from his seat and jogged after Nasia.

What the hell was going on?

Why was she playing the victim?

$$\text{❧} \quad 13 \quad \text{❧}$$

B*reathe.*
In.
Out.

Nasia chanted in her mind. She didn't want to be seen crying in public over a man. She rushed out of the Farmhouse Diner.

The crisp air was comforting as she inhaled it.

She had left the café, needing to get out. She had decided to go for a walk to see if it helped clear her thoughts.

Never would she have thought she'd been walking down Main Street and see Stan having lunch with his ex-wife.

"I guess she wins," Nasia muttered. Crying

wasn't going to fix it. Her heart was shattered. She had been ready to give Stan her everything.

If he wanted to go back to his lying, cheating ex-wife, then that was his business. Now she agreed with her sister, anger filling her.

He should have been man enough to tell her himself.

Nasia folded her arms in front of her and stalked away from the restaurant.

"Nasia!" Stan shouted from behind her.

She ignored him, increasing her pace. She'd go back to her café, finish up what she was doing, then go home to break open a bottle of wine and a tub of ice cream.

Today called for both.

"Nasia." He was right behind her. He snagged her arm and spun her around. "Wait a minute."

"Go back to your wife, Stan." She narrowed her gaze on him, snatching her arm from him.

"What the hell is that supposed to mean?" he snapped.

"She told me that you two are getting back together, but I would have thought you would have had the balls to tell me instead of sending her." Nasia pointed to the Farmhouse Diner.

"We're not getting back together." He ran a trembling hand through his hair. "I don't know why she's talking to you or spreading lies, but that is not happening."

"Well, you two were looking mighty cozy." She had stood outside the window for moments staring at the two of them smiling at each other. Nasia hadn't even realized her feet were carrying her into the restaurant until she'd stood inside next to their table.

"You're a fine one to talk," he growled.

He took her arm and moved her out of the way of a couple of women walking down the sidewalk. They cast a worried glance at Nasia and Stan and moved on.

"What hell are you talking about?" Had he hit his head on something at work? Nothing he was saying was making sense.

"I saw you with that man outside your house."

She paused and stared at him. Her pulse pounded in her ears. She closed her eyes for a moment, then opened them. "Say again?"

"I came by your house last week to surprise you and follow you to the café when I saw you kissing a man then leading him into your house." He rested his hands on his hips, glaring at her.

"That's why you haven't taken my calls and have

been avoiding me?" She wasn't proud to admit that a couple days she'd waited at his house waiting for him to come home from the ranch, but he never did. She assumed he was staying at the ranch, but after seeing him with Victoria, she was unsure where he'd been staying.

"I can't do another cheater, Nasia."

Her head jerked back as if she'd been slapped. Nasia took a step away from him. Did he just call her a cheater?

"And you did nothing? Didn't go to the house and question what you thought you saw?" she asked quietly.

"What for? I know what I saw."

Her anger exploded.

"That was Aleka!" she cried out. She stepped forward and shoved him away from her. "My sister. My identical twin, or did you forget? It wasn't me."

"Wait, what?" The color drained from his face. His Adam's apple bobbed up and down. "Your sister?"

"Did you forget I told you we are identical twins?" The tears flowed down her cheeks. She lost the battle to hold them back. "She ended up coming down to Shady Springs to meet up with her friends.

That's who you saw. I was at the café to prep since I was going to be gone for a few days."

She spun around and took off, unable to look at him.

"Nasia, please stop." Desperation was in his voice. He reached for her, taking her by the shoulder.

She paused, uncaring who saw her openly crying. He gently guided her around to face him.

"Baby, I didn't mean it. I know what I saw and I just…" He clamored for words.

"You immediately put me in the box with your ex-wife." She sniffled. Nasia shrugged, backing away from Stan. That hurt worse than him mistaking her for her twin. If he had come to her, she would have cleared up the mistaken identify and they could have worked past that. Instead, he had grouped her with Victoria. "After everything I did to try to show you that I loved you, this is how you treat me."

"You love me?" His eyes widened in disbelief.

He reached up to touch her chin, but she jerked away from him. There was no way she could allow him to keep touching her. She was only so strong, and her body was already responding to him.

If she stayed in his embrace, she'd give in to him.

She had to resist.

She would never be anyone's second choice.

"Yeah, but don't worry about it. I'll get over it. Go back to your wife." Nasia spun around and stalked away from him. Her vision was blurred with tears. She blinked, allowing them to continue to stream down her cheeks.

What little of her heart remained, shattered completely.

STAN CLOSED THE DOOR TO RINGO'S STALL. The horse snorted, coming to poke this head through the door. Stan gave it one last rub.

At the moment, the only company that tolerated him was that of the equine type.

Nasia's words echoed in his head, even a week later.

Yeah, but don't worry about it. I'll get over it. Go back to your wife.

He had truly fucked up. Here it was he'd had the love of a good woman and he'd thrown it all away due to his own insecurities.

"I see that you have been staying at the ranch lately," Parker's voice sounded behind him.

Stan looked over his shoulder at the elder Brooks brother.

"There's been much to do around here." Stan cleared his throat. He gave Ringo one more pat and turned away.

"There's plenty of men working this ranch to help. You don't have to do it all." Parker tilted his head to the side and studied him. Under that low-brim Stetson of his, those eyes appeared to see everything. "You sure that's all it's been?"

"Maybe." Stan moved toward him and blew out a deep breath.

Parker fell in step with him. He had a limp left over from his bull riding days. A bad accident had retired the bull rider earlier than expected.

They walked in silence, exiting the barn.

"Want to talk about it?" Parker asked.

They ambled over to the fence that surrounded the corral where Rashad was working with a new colt. The Blazing Eagle Ranch always ensured they had fresh horses around for the back-breaking work that was required of all the employees.

Stan leaned against the fence and shook his head. "Not sure it will do any good. I truly fucked up."

"Ah, so woman problems," Parker murmured. "You and Nasia?"

Stan would be surprised that Parker knew about Nasia, but then again, Wade knew of her, so that meant the middle brother would have shared with his brothers.

"Yeah." Stan blew out a deep breath watching the colt's antics. He was as stubborn one, but Rashad was a master of breaking new horses in. He had a way about him that the animals responded to.

"I was happy to hear you had started dating. Why do you think you fucked up?"

Stan removed his hat and combed through his hair. He grimaced, feeling how damp it was.

"Well, you know what happened between me and Victoria." He began the story and ended with him at the diner and being confronted by Nasia.

Parker didn't say a word and allowed him to get it off his chest.

"Shit." Parker cursed. He turned and glanced at Stan. He reached out and rested a hand on Stan's shoulder. "Look, you know I'm your friend and love you like a brother. My advice, get down on your knees and grovel at Nasia's feet to beg for forgiveness."

Stan snorted.

His friend wasn't saying anything he didn't already know.

The hurt on Nasia's face when she realized that he had compared her to his ex-wife just about brought him to his knees. When she'd turned and walked away without looking at him, it had left him gutted.

He didn't know if he could repair the damage that was done.

"I don't even know if she'd take me back." He sighed.

It also didn't help that Victoria had gone to her café and told her how they'd spoken several times about getting back together. So there was already doubt in Nasia's mind, then him not returning her calls and avoiding her solidified what his conniving ex-wife had told her.

"I just don't know how I can make it up to her. She knew how badly I was hurt by Victoria. She'd done everything in her power to show me how she wasn't anything like Victoria, and I ignored all the signs and only saw one thing."

"How did you forget she was a twin? I mean, you all did talk about family in between, you know..." Parker elbowed him playfully.

"Yes, I know she's a twin. I've never met her sister in person. Just saw pictures of them, but all I can say is that night, my brain malfunctioned. It took me back to the day I walked in on Victoria, and I ..."

He shook his head, unable to finish his train of thought.

"What you need to do is share this with Nasia. One thing I've learned over the years, is honesty is the best key. Put it all on the table, and if she accepts, then you need to make sure you show her how much you love her." Parker paused and leaned against the fence, his gaze locked on Stan. "You do love her, right?"

"Yes, I do. More than anything in the world."

That felt good to get off his chest. He hadn't even shared it with her, and now it may be too late. She had said she'd loved him.

In past tense.

His heart cracked thinking that she would no longer love him.

"Then take your sorry ass from my ranch and go to your woman. Your mood is affecting the horses in the barn." Parker chuckled.

Stan smiled, appreciating his friend was trying to comfort him.

"Yes, sir." Stan gave Parker a salute and pushed away from the fence. He marched toward where his truck was parked, determined to win his woman back.

He didn't care what he would have to do, Nasia was going to hear him out.

＊ 14 ＊

"Aren't you glad your little sister is here to take care of you?" Aleka teased.

She had come back to Shady Springs to keep Nasia company. After her confrontation with Stan, Nasia just hadn't felt like doing anything.

She was a mess.

Aleka refused to have her moping around by herself. She'd arrived in her normal fashion, blowing into the house. She'd forced Nasia to shower, put clothes on, and do her hair. Then she'd dragged Nasia from the house and to the grocery store.

"I'm glad to see you whenever we can," Nasia murmured, staring out the passenger window. The town went by in a blur. She didn't see any of it.

All she saw was Stan.

The pained expression on his face when she'd screamed at him that it had been her sister he'd witnessed.

How could he just shut her down?

He hadn't even wanted to fight for her?

"Good. I'm going to cook you a delicious meal, then we are going to binge Netflix and eat ice cream," Aleka rambled.

"Sounds fun." Nasia cleared her throat. She would allow Aleka to spoil her. It was second nature for them.

When they were younger, they'd joked about twin powers. There was a special connection where they sensed certain feelings in each other. Their parents always thought they were crazy when they shared this with them. It wasn't anything like reading minds, but they had a strong bond where they could just tell when the other was sad or happy.

"We are home," Aleka announced. She parked the vehicle outside the garage and killed the engine. She glanced in the rearview mirror. "Who is that?"

Nasia turned around and peered through the back window and froze.

Stan.

His new truck came to park behind Aleka's.

Nasia's gaze met Aleka's shocked one.

"What is he doing here?" Nasia murmured.

"Is that the infamous Stan?" Aleka practically growled.

Nasia nodded.

Aleka flew from the car before Nasia could even react.

"Crap," Nasia muttered. She exited the vehicle to see Aleka standing near the trunk of her ride with her arms folded in front of her chest.

Stan sat in his truck staring at the both of them. She went to stand by her sister, who was practically fuming.

Stan's door opened, and he stepped out of his truck. His gaze flickered between the two of them then landed on her.

"Nasia, can we talk?" he asked.

Her gaze greedily took him in. He was dressed in his flannel shirt, jeans, and shitkickers. His head was free of his Stetson, showcasing his dark hair combed away from his face.

"Oh, so now you can tell us apart," Aleka fumed.

"Aleka..." Nasia grabbed her sister's arm. Without a doubt, Aleka would stand up for her and fight her battles, but this was one that she needed to do.

"I deserved that." Stan walked to the front of his

truck and faced off with both of them. "I'm not perfect and I'm coming here to beg for your sister to forgive me."

Nasia's heart skipped a beat.

He was here to beg?

"What you did was shady. How do you just cut her off like that? I had to deal with your fuck-up and come back down here to—"

"Aleka," Nasia snapped, moving in front of her sister. The mama bear in her sister was coming out. She rested a hand on Aleka's cheek. "I got this, sis. Go in the house."

"Hell naw. Anything he got to say, he can say in front of me." Aleka stepped back and leaned against her car.

Nasia turned back to Stan whose wide eyes were locked on her twin. He settled them on Nasia.

"She can be little protective of me," Nasia admitted.

"I see." He cleared his throat. His voice shook slightly, but he held her gaze. "Nasia, I have to say, I was the biggest asshat in the whole damn state of Colorado."

Aleka snorted.

Nasia ignored her.

Stan moved to stand before her. He tipped her chin up, forcing her to stare up into his eyes.

"You know my history, and I have to say it came back to me, blinding me to the truth. Now seeing you two standing together, I can see that you're identical, but I can tell the difference. My mind blanked on the fact that you're a twin. I just got so caught up in my feelings, thinking the woman I loved was kissing another man."

"You love me?" She rested her hands on his chest, unable to keep herself from touching him.

His hands skated along her body and came to rest on her waist.

"More than life itself. I know we haven't been together long, but everything about you is perfect for me. The night you brought me back here and, um…" His gaze flicked over her shoulder to her sister.

"I know the night you are speaking of," she said, saving him the embarrassment.

"Sounds like I need to hear what happened that night," Aleka joked.

"Shut it, sis. It's none of your business." Nasia looked over her shoulder at her sister whose eyebrows were elevated.

She turned back to Stan, feeling herself softening toward him. His tortured look had her heart melting.

He cupped her cheek with his large hand, his eyes boring into hers.

"I was so angry, I was seeing red. I needed time to process everything. I had planned to come and see you so we can talk."

"We should have spoken right away. I didn't even know my sister had a guy at my house until I had returned back to Shady Springs after going to Denver."

He closed his eyes briefly then opened them again.

"Baby, please forgive me. There have never been any plans for me to get back with Victoria. She's been lying to you."

"But you two were laughing and smiling at each other—"

He placed a finger to her lips to silence her.

"I went to the diner alone. She showed up out of nowhere, having tracked me down and invited herself to my table." He paused, trailing his finger along her bottom lip, his gaze locked on it.

She snuck out her tongue to moisten it since it suddenly felt dry.

"She was telling me about her father who had recently retired. I'm cool with her parents still, and her father is a great guy."

"Too bad his daughter—"

He pressed his finger to her lips again.

"Anyway, that was all. Nothing to it. As much as she wants to get back with me, I can't."

"Why?" she breathed. The desire to hear the words again was strong. She leaned into him, waiting to hear those three magical words.

"Because I'm in love with you and I'm willing to do whatever I must to get back in your good graces."

Nasia stood up on her toes and brought his head down to hers. Their lips met in a deep, passionate kiss. Nasia wrapped her arms around his neck to hold him place.

There was no other person she would rather be with. She was kidding herself if she thought she would be able to stay away from this man.

She tore her mouth from his. "Stan Larsen..." She stared up into his clear blue eyes, searching them. She saw nothing but a tortured man baring his soul to her. "Don't you ever doubt me again. Do you hear me? I love you so much."

"Baby, I won't. I promise." He brought her in close.

She rested her head against his chest, breathing in his scent that she'd missed so much.

"Okay, you two. All is forgiven." Aleka chuckled.

"Stan, it's nice to finally meet you. If you want to be in my good graces, you'll carry these groceries in, and I'll cook both of you dinner."

"Yes, ma'am." Stan grinned at Aleka. He settled another kiss on Nasia's lips and stepped back. "Let me get the bags before your sister scratches my eyes out."

Nasia barked a laugh and moved out the way.

Today was looking up. Dinner, a movie, and spending time with her two favorite people meant this day was ending on a great note.

EPILOGUE

"Why are you awake?" Nasia grumbled. Her naked body was lying flush against his.

Stan stared down at his beautiful new wife. She opened an eye and glared at him. "Are you smiling? It's too early to be grinning like that."

He barked a laugh and kissed her cheek.

Their relationship continued in its whirlwind fashion. After he'd received her forgiveness, they had moved in with each other within a month. A week later, he'd popped the big question, and now here it was, two months later, and they were married.

He'd fallen in love with not only her but her family. Her father had given his blessing to ask for his daughter's hand in marriage.

"How can I sleep when I have the most beautiful woman in the world as my wife?" He picked up her hand to stare at her diamond bridal set on her ring finger. He kissed it and rested her hand on his chest.

"Sounds like you want something." Nasia snorted.

He was quickly learning his wife was not a morning person while on vacation. They were on their honeymoon in the Bahamas at a private inclusive resort.

Their suite was fit for a royalty. The open doors near the bed led to a private oasis that included a soaking tub for two. The area was surrounded by privacy curtains and a small garden. Their spacious master bedroom housed a king-sized bed in an open-concept sitting area that had everything they needed, even a full bar. In the two days they had been there, they'd barely left the bed, their marriage officially consummated.

"Only you." He dropped another kiss to her still swollen lips.

Stan couldn't remember ever being so happy. Life was good. Victoria had finally got the message that he wasn't coming back to her. Last he had heard, she had packed up and moved to Colorado Springs for a new job.

He stood from the bed and scooped Nasia up.

"Stan!" she shrieked.

Her arms came to rest around his neck as he walked toward the patio.

"What?" he asked, trying to appear innocent.

"What time is it?"

"Does it matter? We are on our honeymoon." The scent of the gardens accosted him. He breathed in the beautiful scent and stepped down into the warm water.

Nasia had finally found the perfect person as her assistant manager. Sally was her name and had been a homemaker for years. Now her kids were all grown and out of the house, she was ready to return to the workforce. Nasia's café was doing so well, she had added on a few more full-timers and was thinking of opening another café a town over.

He couldn't be more proud of her.

He settled them into the water with Nasia straddling him. His cock took notice that his wife's opening was near.

"You're right," Nasia murmured. She pressed a hard kiss to his lips. "This is the best way to wake up."

"We're about to make it even better." He slipped his hand beneath the water's surface and gripped the base of his cock, guiding the tip to her opening.

"Hmmm…I love you, Mr. Larsen." Nasia moaned, impaling herself on his cock. She slid down until he was fully sheathed into her warmness.

"I love you, too, Mrs. Larsen." He groaned, settled his hands on her ass, and held her in place. Her full breasts rested on his chest.

"I just can't get enough of you," she gasped. She lifted and slid back down on him. Her gaze met his and held it as they moved in sync with each other. "I'm so happy."

"Good."

Stan had made it his mission to please his wife. Never again would there be doubts in the back of his mind whether she loved him.

Together, they had built a strong relationship.

Nothing would ever come between them again.

The End

A NOTE FROM THE AUTHOR

Dear reader,

I hope you enjoyed Stan and Nasia's story as much as I did. These two are amazing together and I'm so happy I got to tell their love story. This story flowed so well I wrote it in ten days!

Don't forget to leave a review. Want more cowboys? Make sure you leave me a review saying this!

Love,

Peyton

HARD TO FORGET
BLAZING EAGLE RANCH 5

Trouble follows her wherever she goes. He's a man willing to prove his love for her.

Nykee Nash returned home to Shady Springs a changed woman. No longer was she the juvenile delinquent who committed crimes and broke the law. Nykee had paid her debt to society and wanted to move on with her life. She threw herself into her new passion and was the happiest she had ever been.

Until Karl sauntered through the door of her newly established business.

Around Karl, Nykee began to live again.

Karl Tanis didn't know what hit him. One look in Nykee's warm brown eyes, and he was a goner. Karl had heard of her past but believed everyone deserves a second chance. He had spent most of his life working a ranch and was no stranger to hard work.

He was up for the challenge to wrangle in Nykee's heart.

She's stubborn, but he's confident he will win her over. But with a twist of fate, everything they had came crashing down around them.

Nykee doesn't want him anywhere near her now, refusing to let him help fight her battles. There's no way he is leaving her alone. He will not give up on their love because she would be hard to forget...

The next book in the Blazing Eagle Ranch is available now!

ABOUT THE AUTHOR

USA TODAY bestselling author, Peyton Banks, is the alter ego of a city girl who is a romantic at heart. Her mornings consist of coffee and daydreaming up the next steamy romance book ideas. She loves spinning romantic tales of hot alpha males and the women they love. Make sure you check her out!

Sign up for Peyton's Newsletter to find out the latest releases, giveaways and news! Visit www.peyton banks.com/newsletter to sign up!

Want to know the latest about Peyton Banks? Follow her online:

Current Free Short Story

Summer Escape

Book Boyfriend Dating Agency

Surgeon Book Boyfriend

Silver Creek Ranch (Shared World)

Wrangling Her Cowboy

Lunchtime Chronicles (Peyton's)

Polish Boy

Thick & Beefy

Rich & Decadent

The Keith Brothers

Mr. Hotness

Mr. Arrogant

Blazing Eagle Ranch Series

Back in the Saddle

Knockin' the Boots

Roping a Cowboy

Country at Heart

Cowboy, Take Me Away

Hard to Forget

<u>Special Weapons & Tactics Series</u>

Dirty Tactics (Special Weapons & Tactics 1)

Dirty Ballistics (Special Weapons & Tactics 2)

Dirty Operations (Special Weapons & Tactics 3)

Dirty Alliance (Special Weapons & Tactics 4)

Dirty Justice (Special Weapons & Tactics 5)

Dirty Trust (Special Weapons & Tactics 6)

Dirty Secrets (Special Weapons & Tactics 7)

Dirty Ultimatum (Special Weapons & Tactics 8)

<u>SWAT boxset, books 1-3</u>

<u>Trust & Honor Series (BWWM)</u>

Dallas

Dalton

<u>A Langdale Christmas</u>

The Christmas Secret

The Christmas Wish

The Christmas Gift

<u>Interracial Romances (BWWM)</u>

Pieces of Me

Hard Love

Retain Me

Silent Deception

<u>African American Romance</u>

Breaking The Rules

<u>Mafia Romance</u>

Unexpected Allies (The Tokhan Bratva 1)

www.ingramcontent.com/pod-product-compliance
Lightning Source LLC
Chambersburg PA
CBHW051431130726
47987CB00005B/2000